The Spell Sword

G·K
Hall
&C͉o

*Also by Marion Zimmer Bradley
in Large Print:*

Darkover Landfall

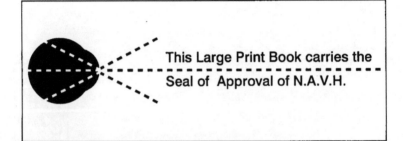

This Large Print Book carries the
Seal of Approval of N.A.V.H.

The Spell Sword

Marion Zimmer Bradley

G.K. Hall & Co. • Thorndike, Maine

1605 1276

Published in 2000 by arrangement with DAW Books, Inc.

G.K. Hall Large Print Science Fiction Series.

The text of this Large Print edition is unabridged.
Other aspects of the book may vary from the original edition.

Set in 16 pt. Plantin by Minnie B. Raven.

Printed in the United States on permanent paper.

Library of Congress Cataloging-in-Publication Data

Bradley, Marion Zimmer.
    The spell sword / Marion Zimmer Bradley.
       p.   cm.
     ISBN 0-7838-9066-4 (lg. print : hc : alk. paper)
     1. Darkover (Imaginary place) — Fiction.   2. Life on other planets
— Fiction.   3. Large type books.   I. Title.
PS3552.R228 S65   2000
813'.54—dc21   00-036987

Jefferson-Madison
Regional Library
Charlottesville, Virginia

This one is for
CARADOC.

Chapter
ONE

He had followed a dream, and it had brought him here to die.

Half conscious, he lay on the rocks and thin moss of the mountain crevasse, and in his dazed state it seemed to him that the girl he had seen in that earlier dream stood before him. *You ought to be laughing,* Andrew Carr said to her imagined face. *If it weren't for you I'd be halfway across the galaxy by now.*

Not lying here half dead on a frozen lump of dust at the edge of nowhere.

But she was not laughing. It seemed that she was standing at the very edge of the lip of rock, the bitter mountain wind blowing her thin blue draperies about her slender body, her hair bright red and gleaming, long about her delicate features. Just as he had seen her before, in the dream, but she was not laughing. Her delicate face looked pale and stern.

And it seemed that she spoke, although the dying man knew — *knew* — that her voice could not be anything but the echo of the wind in his fevered brain.

"Stranger, stranger, I did not mean you harm; it was none of my calling or my doing that brought you to this pass! True, I called you — or rather I called to anyone who could hear me, and it was you. But those above us both know that I meant you no ill! The winds, the storms, these are not under my command. I will do what I may to save you, but I have no power in these mountains."

It seemed to Andrew Carr that he flung angry words back at her. *I'm mad,* he thought, *or maybe already dead, lying here exchanging insults with a ghost-girl.*

"You say you called me? But what of the others in my ship? You called them too, perhaps? And brought them here to die in the crosswinds of the Hellers? Does death by wholesale give you any pleasure, you ghoul-girl?"

"That isn't fair!" Her imagined words were like a cry of anguish and her ghost-face on the wind twisted as if she were about to weep. "I did not call them; they came in the path where their work and their destiny led. Only you had the choice to come, or not to come, because of my call; you chose to come, and to share whatever fate their destiny held for them. I will save you if I can; for them, their time is ended and their destiny was never at my disposal. You I can save, if you will hear me, but you must rouse yourself. Rouse yourself!" It was like a wild cry of despair. "You will die if you lie here longer! Rouse yourself and take shelter, for the winds and the storms are not mine to command. . . ."

Andrew Carr opened his eyes and blinked. As he had known all along, he was alone, lying battered on the mountain ledges in the wreckage of the mapping plane. The girl — if she had ever been there at all — was gone.

Rouse yourself and take shelter, for the winds and the storms are not mine to command. That was, of course, a damn good idea, if he could manage it. Shelter. Where he lay, under a fragment of the smashed cabin of the mapping plane, was no place to meet the bitter night of this strange planet. He'd been warned about the weather here when he first came to Cottman IV — only a lunatic would stay out in the nights during the storm season.

He fought again, with a last desperate effort, to free the ankle which was caught, like the leg of a trapped animal, in twisted metal. This time he felt the metal crumple and give a little, and, although the ripping pain grew greater, tearing skin and flesh, he wrenched grimly at the caught foot in the darkness. Now he could move enough to bend over and move the leg with his hands. Torn clothing and torn flesh were slippery with blood which was already beginning to stiffen in the icy cold. When he touched the jagged metal his bare hands burned like fire, but now he could guide the wounded leg upward, avoiding the worst jagged edges of metal. Now, with a gasp of mingled agony and relief, his foot was free; blood-covered, boot and clothing torn, cut to the bone, but free; he was trapped no longer. He struggled to his feet, to be beaten again to his knees by a gust of the icy, sleet-laden wind that whipped around a corner of the rock-ledge.

Crawling, to present less body surface to the wind, he crept inside the cabin of the mapping plane. It was swaying dangerously in the battering wind, and he immediately abandoned any thought of taking shelter in here. If the wind got any worse, the whole damn thing would catapult down at least a thousand feet into the invisible valley below. Part of it, he thought, had already gone with the first crash. But finding himself still alive, beyond all expectations, he had to be sure there was no other survivor.

Stanforth was dead, of course. He must have been killed in the very first shock; nothing could survive with that gaping hole in its forehead. Andrew shut his eyes against the ghastly sight of the man's brains frozen and spilled all over his face. The two mappers — one was called Mattingly; he had never known the other's name — were twisted limp on the floor, and when he cautiously crawled across the jiggling balance of the cabin to find if any spark of life remained in either, it was only to feel the bodies already cold and stiffened in rigor. There was no sign of the pilot. He must have gone down with the nose of the plane, into that awful chasm below them.

So he was alone. Cautiously, Andrew backed out of the cabin; then, steeling himself, reentered it again. There was food in the plane — not much, a day's rations, lunches, Mattingly's hoard of sweets and candies, which he had so generously passed around and which they had all laughingly refused; emergency supplies in a marked panel behind the door. He dragged them all out, and, shaking with terror, set himself to wrench Mattingly's huge topcoat off the stiffening corpse. It made his stomach turn — *robbing the dead!* — but Mattingly's topcoat, a great expensive fur thing, was of no use to its owner and it might mean the difference between life and death in the terrible oncoming night.

When he edged out of the hideously shaking cabin for the last time, he was trembling and sick, and his torn, cut leg, no longer mercifully numb, was beginning to tear at him with claws of pain. He carefully backed away against the inner edge of the cliff, piling his hard-won provisions close to the rock-face.

It occurred to him that he should make one final essay inside the plane. Stanforth, Mattingly, and the nameless other man had carried identification, their disks from the Terran Empire Service. If he lived, if he came again to the Port, this would serve as proof of their death and mean something to their kinfolk. Wearily, he dragged himself forward.

And she was there again, the girl, the ghost, the ghoul who had brought him here, white with terror, standing directly in his way. Her mouth seemed drawn with screaming.

"No! No!"

Involuntarily he stepped back. He knew she was not there, he knew she was only air, but he stepped back and his lamed foot crumpled under him; he fell against the rock-cliff as a gust of wind struck it, howling like a damned thing. The girl was gone, was nowhere, but before he could drag himself to his feet again, there was a great howling blast of wind and icy sleet, a sound like a thunderclap. With a final rattling, rocking clash the cabin of the wrecked plane slid free from its resting place and overbalanced, tipped, slid down the rocks, and crashed into the chasm below. There was a great roar like an avalanche, like the end of the world. Andrew clung, gasping, to the face of the cliff, his fingers trying to freeze to the rocks.

Then it quieted and there was only the soft roaring of the storm and the snow-spray, and Andrew huddled in Mattingly's fur topcoat, waiting for his heart to quiet to normal.

The girl had saved him again. She had kept him from going into the cabin, that last time.

Nonsense, he thought. *Unconsciously I must have known it was ready to go.*

He shelved the thought for later pondering. Just now he had escaped, by the second in a series of miracles, but he was still very far from safe.

If that wind could blow a plane right off a cliff, it could blow him, too, he reasoned. He had to find some safer place to rest, shelter.

Cautiously, clinging to the inner part of the

ledge, he crept along the wall. Ten feet beyond where he lay, in one direction, it narrowed to nothing and ended in a dark rock-fall, slippery with the falling sleet. Painfully, his foot clawing anguish, he retraced his steps. The darkness seemed to be thickening and the sleet turning to white, soft thick snow. Aching and tired, Andrew wished he could lie down, wrap himself in the fur coat, and sleep there. But to sleep was death, his bones knew it, and he resisted the temptation, dragging himself along the cliff-ledge in the opposite direction. He had to avoid the fragments of torn metal which had held him trapped. Once he gave his good leg a painful shin-blow on a concealed rock which bent him over, moaning in pain.

But at last he had traversed the full length of the ledge, and at the far end, he found that it widened, sloping gently upward to a flat space on which thick underbrush clung, root-fast to the mountainside. Looking up in the thickening darkness, Andrew nodded. The clustered, thick foliage would resist the wind — it had evidently been rooted there for years. Anything which could grow here would have to be able to hang on hard against wind and storm, tempest and blizzard. Now, if his lamed foot would let him haul himself up there . . .

It wasn't easy, burdened with coat and food supplies, his foot torn and bleeding, but before the darkness closed in entirely, he had dragged himself and his small stock of provisions —

crawling, at last, on both hands and one knee —
up beneath the trees, and collapsed in their
shelter. At least here the maddening wind blew a
little less violently, its strength broken by the
boughs. In the emergency supplies there was a
small battery-operated light, and by its pale
glimmer he found concentrated food, a thin
blanket of the "space" kind, which would insu-
late his body heat inside its shelter, and tablets of
fuel.

He rigged the blanket and his own coat into a
rough lean-to, using the thickest crossed branches
to support them, so that he lay in a tiny dugout
scooped beneath the tree-roots and boughs,
where only occasional snow-spray reached him.
Now he wanted nothing more than to collapse
and lie motionless, but before his last strength
left him, he grimly cut away the frozen trouser-
leg and the remnants of his boot from his damaged leg. It hurt more than he had ever dreamed
anything could hurt, to smear it with the anti-
septic in the emergency kit and bandage it tightly
up again, but somehow he managed it, although
he heard himself moaning like a wild animal. He
dropped at last, exhausted beyond weariness, in
his burrow, reaching out finally for one of
Mattingly's candies. He forced himself to chew
it, knowing that the sugar would warm his shivering body, but in the very act of swallowing, he
fell into an exhausted, deathlike sleep.

For a long time, his sleep was like that of the
dead, dark and without dreams, a total blotting-

out of mind and will. And then for a long time he was dimly aware of fever and pain, of the raging of the storm outside. After it diminished, still in the darkening fever-drowse, he woke raging with thirst, and crawled outside, breaking icicles from the edge of his shelter to suck them, staggering away from the shelter to answer the needs of his body. Then he dropped exhausted inside his hollowed-out shelter to swallow a little food and fell again into deep pain-wracked sleep.

When he woke again it was morning, and he was clear-headed, seeing clear light and hearing only a faint murmur of wind on the heights. The storm was over; his foot and leg still pained him, but endurably. When he sat up to change the bandages, he saw the wound was clean and unfestered. Above him the great blood-red sun of Cottman IV lay low in the sky, slowly climbing the heights. He crept to the edge and looked down into the valley, which lay wrapped in mist below. It was wild, lonesome country and seemed untouched by any human hands.

Yet this was an inhabited world, a world peopled by humans who were, as far as he knew, indistinguishable from Earthmen. He had somehow survived the crash which had wrecked the Mapping and Exploring plane; it should not be wholly impossible, somehow, to make his way back to the spaceport again. Perhaps the natives would be friendly and help him, although he had to admit it didn't seem too likely.

Still, while there was life there was hope . . .

and he still had his life. Men had been lost, before this, in the wild and unexplored areas of strange worlds, and had come out of it alive, living to tell about it at Empire Central back on Earth. So that his first task was to get his leg back in walking shape, and his second, to get out of these mountains. *Hellers.* Good name for them. They were hellish all right. Crosswinds, updrafts, downdrafts, storms blowing up out of nowhere — the plane wasn't made that could fly through them unscathed in bad weather. He wondered how the natives got across them. Pack-mules or some local equivalent, he thought. Anyway, there would be passes, roads, trails.

As the sun rose higher, the mists cleared and he could look down into the valleys below. Most of the slopes were tree-clad, but far below in the valley a river ran, and across it there was some darkening which could only be a bridge. So he wasn't in entirely uninhabited country, after all. There were blotches which might well be plowed lands, squared fields, gardens, a pleasant and peaceful countryside, with smoke rising from chimneys and houses — but very far away; and between the cultivated lands and the cliffside where Andrew clung were seemingly endless leagues of chasms and foothills and crags.

Somehow, though, he'd get down there, and then back to the spaceport. And then, damn it, off this ghastly inhospitable planet where he never should have come in the first place, and having come, should have left again within forty-eight hours. Well, he'd go now.

And what about the girl?

Damn the girl. She never existed. She was a fever-dream, a ghost, a symbol of his own loneliness. . . .

Lonely. I've always been alone, on a dozen worlds.

Probably every lonely man dreams that some-day he will arrive at a world where someone is waiting, someone who will stretch out a hand to him, and speak to something inside, saying, "I am here. We are together. . . ."

There had been women, of course. Women in every port — what was the old saying, starting with sailors and transferred to spacemen, always a new one in every port? And there were men who thought that state of affairs was enviable, he knew.

But none of them had been the right woman, and at heart he knew all the things the Psych Division had told him. They ought to know. You look for perfection in a woman to protect your-self against a real relationship. You take refuge in fantasies to avoid looking at the hard realities of life. And so forth and so on. Some of them even told him that he was unconsciously homosexual and found ordinary sexual affairs unsatisfactory because it wasn't really women he wanted at all, he just couldn't admit it to himself. He'd heard it all, a hundred times, yet the dream remained.

Not just a woman for his bed, but one for his heart and his heart-hungry loneliness. . . .

Maybe that was what the old fortune-teller in the Old Town had been playing on. Maybe so many men shared that romantic dream that she handed it out to everybody, as psi-quacks back on Earth told romantic teenage girls about a tall dark stranger they would surely meet someday.

No. It was a real girl. I saw her and she — she called me.

All right. Think about it now. Get it all straight. . . .

He had come to Cottman IV en route to a new assignment, and it was simply a port of call, one of a series of crossroads worlds where routings were changed in the great network of the Terran Empire. The spaceport was large, as was the Trade City around it, to cater to the spaceport personnel, but it was not an Empire world with established trade, travel, tours. It was, he knew, an inhabited world, but most of it was off limits to Earthmen. He didn't even know what the natives called it. The name on the Empire maps was enough for him, Cottman IV. He hadn't intended to stay there more than forty-eight hours, only long enough to arrange transit to his final destination.

And then, with three others from the Space Service, he had gone into the Old Town. Ship fare got tiresome; it always tasted of machines, with a strong acrid taste of spices to cover the pervasive tang of recycled water and hydrocarbons. The food in the Old Town was at least natural, good grilled meat such as he had not had since his last planetside billeting, and fresh fragrant fruits, and he had enjoyed it more than any meal he had tasted in months, with the sweet clear gold-colored wine. And then, out of curiosity, he and his companions had strolled through the marketplace, buying souvenirs, fingering strange rough-textured fabrics and soft furs, and then he had come to the booth of the fortune-teller, and out of amused curiosity he had paused at her words.

"Someone is waiting for you. I can show you the face of your destiny, stranger. Would you see the face of the one who waits for you?"

He had never dreamed that it was more than a standard pitch for a few coins; amused, laughing, he had given the wrinkled old woman the coins she asked for, and followed her inside her small awning-covered canvas booth. Inside she had looked into her crystal — strange how on every world he had ever known the crystal ball was the chosen instrument of pretended far-seeing — and then, without a word, shoved the ball toward him. Still half in laughter, half in disgust, ready to walk away, Andrew had bent to see the pretty face, the shining red hair. *A pitch for a high-class call-girl,* he thought cynically, and was prepared to ask what the old madam was charging for the girl that day, and if she made a special price for Earthmen. Then the girl in the crystal raised her eyes and met Andrew's, and . . .

And it happened. There were no words for it. He stood there, half-crouched and unmoving over the crystal, so long that his neck, unheeded, was stabbed with cramp in the muscles.

19

She was very young, and she seemed to be both frightened and in pain. It seemed that she cried out to him for help that only he could give, and that she touched, deliberately, some secret thing known only to both of them. But he could not, later, understand what it had been, only that she called to him, that she needed him desperately. . . .

And then her face was gone and his head was aching. He gripped at the edge of the table, shaking, desperate to call her back. "Where is she? Who is she?" he demanded, and the old woman turned up a blank, frowning face. "No, now, how do I know what you saw, off-worlder? I saw nothing and no one, and others are waiting. You must go now."

He had stumbled out, blank with despair.

She called to me. She needs me. She is here. . . .

And I am leaving in six hours.

It hadn't been exactly easy to break his contract and stay, but it hadn't been all that hard either. Places on the world to which he was going were in high demand, and there wouldn't be more than three days' delay in filling his position. He'd have to accept two downgrades in seniority, but he didn't care. On the other hand, as Personnel told him, volunteers for Cottman IV weren't easy to find. The climate was bad, there was almost no trade, and although the pay was good, no career man really wanted to exile himself way out here on the fringes of the Empire on a planet which stubbornly refused to have any

20

dealings with them except for leasing the spaceport itself. They offered him a choice of work in the computer center, or in Mapping and Exploring, which was high-risk, high-pay work. For some reason, the natives of this world had never mapped it, and the Terran Empire felt that presenting them with finished maps which their native technology could not, or would not, encompass might be a very good thing for public relations between Cottman IV and the Empire.

He chose Mapping and Exploring. He already knew — in the first week he had seen every girl and woman in the spaceport — that she was none of the workers in Medic or Personnel or Dispatch. Mapping and Exploring enjoyed certain concessions which allowed them to go outside the severely limited preserve of the Empire. *Somewhere, somehow, she was out there waiting. . . .*

It was an obsession and he knew it, but somehow he could not break the spell, and didn't want to.

And then, the third time he'd gone out with the mapping plane, the crash . . . and here he was, no closer than ever to his dream girl. If she had ever existed, which he doubted.

Exhausted by the long effect of memory, he crawled back into his shelter to rest. Time enough tomorrow to work out a plan for getting down off the ledge. He ate emergency rations, sucked ice, fell into an uneasy sleep. . . .

She was there again, standing before him, both in and not quite in the little dark shelter, a ghost, a dream, a dark flower, a flame in his heart. . . .

I do not know why it is you I have touched, stranger. I sought for my kinfolk, those who love me and could help me. . . .

Damsel in distress, Andrew thought, *I just bet. What do you want with me?*

Only a look of pain, and a sorrowful twisting of the face.

Who are you? I can't keep calling you ghost-girl.

Callista.

Now I know I'm freaked out, Andrew said to himself. *That's an Earth name.*

I am no Earth sorceress, my powers are of air and fire. . . .

That made no sense. *What do you want with me?*

Just now, only to save the life I unwittingly endangered. And I say to you: avoid the darkened land.

She faded abruptly from sight and hearing, and he was alone, blinking.

"Callista" means simply "beautiful," as I remember, he thought. *Maybe she is simply a symbol of beauty in my mind. But what is the darkened land? And how can she help to save me? Oh, rubbish, I'm treating her as if she were real again.*

Face it. There's no such woman, and if you're going to get out of here, you'll have to go it alone.

And yet, as he lay back to rest and make plans, he found himself trying, again, to call up her face before his eyes. . . .

Chapter
TWO

The storm still raged on the heights, but here in the valley daylight shone through, and lowering sunlight; only the thick anvil-shaped clouds to the west showed where the peaks of the mountains were wrapped in storm.

Damon Ridenow rode with head down, braced against the wind that ripped his riding-cloak, and it felt like flight. As if he fled before a gathering storm. He tried to tell himself, *The weather's getting into my bones, maybe I'm just not as young as I was,* but he knew it was more than that. It was an unease, something stirring, nagging at his mind, something wrong. Something rotten.

He realized that he had been keeping his eyes turned from the low tree-clad hills which lay to the east, and deliberately, trying to break the strange unease, made himself twist in his saddle and look up and down the slopes.

The darkened lands.

Rubbish, he said to himself angrily. There was war there, last year, with the cat-people. Some of his folk were killed and others were driven away, forced to resettle in the Alton country, around the lakes. The cat-people were fierce and cruel, yes, they slaughtered and burned and tormented and left for dead what they could not kill outright. Maybe what he felt was simply the memory of all the suffering there during the war. *My mind is open to the minds of those who suffered. . . .*

No, it was worse than that. The things he'd heard about what the cat-people did.

He glanced behind him. His escort — four swordsmen of the Guard — were beginning to draw together and murmur, and he knew he should call a halt to breathe the horses. One of them spurred and came to his side, and he reined his mount in to look at the man.

"Lord Damon," the Guardsman said, with proper deference — but he looked angry. "Why do we ride as if foemen rode hard at our heels? I have heard no word of war or ambush."

Damon Ridenow forced his pace to slacken slightly, but it was an effort. He wanted to spur his mount hard, to race away for the safety of Armida beyond them. . . .

He said somberly, "I think we *are* pursued, Reidel."

The Guardsman warily swept his eyes from horizon to horizon — it was his trained duty to be wary — but with open skepticism. "Which bush, think you, hides ambush, Lord Damon?"

"That you know no more than I," said Damon, sighing.

The man looked stubborn. He said, "Well, you are a Comyn Lord, and it is your business, and mine to carry out your orders. But there is a limit to what man and horseflesh can do, Lord, and if we are attacked with wearied horses and saddle sores, we will fight the less."

"I suppose you're right," Damon said, sighing. "Call halt if you will, then. Here at least there is little danger of attack in open country."

He was cramped and weary, and glad to dismount, even though the nightmare urgency still beat at him. When the Guard Reidel brought him food, he took it without smiling, and his thanks were absentminded. The Guardsman lingered with the privilege of an old acquaintance.

"Do you still smell danger behind every tree, Lord Damon?"

"Yes, but I can't say why," Damon said, sighing. Afoot he was little more than medium height, a thin pale man with the fire-red hair of a Comyn Lord of the Seven Domains; like most of his kindred he went unarmed except for a dagger, and under his riding-cloak he wore the light tunic of an indoor man, a scholar. The Guardsman was looking at him solicitously.

"You are unused to so much riding, Lord, and in such haste. Was there so much need for it, so swiftly?"

"I do not know," the Comyn Lord said quietly. "But my kinswoman at Armida sent me a message — a guarded one — begging me to come to her with all speed, and she is not of that fearful

25

kind who start at shadows and lie awake nights fearing bandits in the courtyard when her men-folk are away. An urgent summons from the Lady Ellemir is nothing to treat lightly, so I came at once, as I must. It may well be some family trouble, some sickness in her household; but whatever it is, the matter is grave or she could deal with it on her own."

The Guardsman nodded slowly. "I have heard the lady is brave and resourceful," he said, "I have a brother who is a part of her household staff. May I tell my fellows this much, Lord? They may grumble less, if they know it is grave trouble and no whim of your own."

"Tell them and welcome, it is no secret," Damon said, "I would have done so myself, if I had thought to do so."

Reidel grinned. "I know you are no man-driver," he said, "but none of us had heard rumors, and this is not a country any man cares to ride in without need." He was turning away, but Damon kept him, a hand on his sleeve.

"Not a country to ride in without need — what do you mean, Reidel?"

Now that he was asked a direct question, the man fidgeted.

"Unchancy," he said at last, "and bad luck. It lies under a shadow. They call it, now, the darkening lands, and no man will ride there or travel there unless he must, and not even then unless he carries mighty protections."

"Nonsense."

"You may laugh, Lord, you Comyn are protected by the Great Gods."

Damon sighed. "I had not thought to find you
so superstitious, Reidel. You have been a Guardsman for a score of years, you were paxman to my
father. Do you still think we Comyn are otherwise than other men?"

"You are luckier," Reidel said, his teeth
clenched, "but now, when men ride into the
darkening lands, they return no more, or return
with their wits astray. No, Lord, do not laugh at
me, it befell my mother's brother two moons ago.
He rode into the darkened lands to visit a maid
he would make his second wife, having paid
bride-price when she was but nine. He came not
when he was expected, and when they told me he
had gone forever into the shadow, I too laughed
and said he had, no doubt, delayed to bed the girl
and get her with child. Then one night, Lord,
after overstaying his leave a full ten days, he rode
into the Guardroom at Serré late one night. I am
not a fanciful man, Lord, but his face — his face
—" He gave up struggling for words, and said,
"He looked as if he'd been looking straight down
into Zandru's seventh hell. And he said nothing
that made sense, Lord. He raved of great fires,
and of death in the winds, and withered gardens,
and witch-food that took a man's wits, and of
girls who clawed at his soul like cat-hags; and
though they sent for the sorceress, before she
could come to heal his mind, he sank, and died
raving."

"Some sickness in the mountains and foot-hills," Damon said, but Reidel shook his head.

"As you reminded me, Lord, I have been Guardsman in these hills a score of years, and my uncle twoscore. I know the sicknesses that strike men, and this was none of them. Nor do I know any sickness which strikes a man only in one direction. I myself rode a little way into the darkened lands, Lord, and I saw for myself the withered gardens and untended orchards, and the folk who live there now. It is true they live on witch-food, Lord."

Damon interrupted again. "Witch-food? There are no such things as witches, Reidel."

"Call it what you will, but this is no food from grain, root, berry, or wholesome tree, Lord, nor flesh of any living thing. I would not touch a grain of it, and I think this is why I escaped unscathed. I saw it come from the air."

Damon said, "Those who know their business can prepare food from things which look inedible, Reidel, and it is wholesome. A matrix technician — how can I explain this? He breaks down the chemical matter which cannot be eaten with safety, and changes its structure so that it can be digested and will nourish. It is not sufficient to sustain life for many months, but it will keep life for a little while in urgency. This I can do myself, and there is no witchery to it."

Reidel frowned. "Sorcery of your starstone —"

"Sorcery be damned," Damon said testily. "A skill."

"Then why can no one do it but you Comyn?"

He sighed. "I cannot play upon the lute; my ears and fingers have neither the inborn talent nor the training. But you, Reidel, were born with the ear, and the fingers were trained in childhood, and so you make music as you wish. So it is with this. The Comyn are born with talent, as it might be a talent for music, and in childhood we are trained to change the structure of matter with the help of those matrix stones. I can do only a few small things; those well-trained can do much. Perhaps someone has been experimenting with such imitation food in those lands, and not knowing his skill full well, has wrought poison instead, a poison which sets men's wits running wild. But this is a matter for one of the Keepers. Why has no one brought this to them for their mending, Reidel?"

"Say what you like," the Guardsman said, and his clenched and stubborn face said volumes. "The darkened lands lie under some evil, and men of goodwill should avoid them. And now, if it pleases you, Lord, we should be a-horse again if we would reach Armida before nightfall. For even if we stay clear of the darkening lands, this is no road to ride by night."

"You are right," said Damon, and mounted, waiting while his escort gathered again. He had plenty to think about. He had, indeed, heard rumors about the lands at the fringes of the cat-country, but nothing, as yet, like this. Was it all superstition, rumor based on the gossip of the ig-

29

norant? No; Reidel was no fanciful man, nor was his uncle, a hard-bitten soldier for twenty years, any man to fall prey to vague shadows. Something very tangible had killed him; and he'd have bet the old fellow would have taken a lot of killing.

They had topped the summit of the hill, and Damon looked down into the valley, alert for any sign of ambush; for his sense of being watched, pursued, had grown to an obsession by now. This would be a good place for an ambush, as they came up over the hill.

But the road and the valley lay bare before them in the cloudy sunlight, and Damon frowned, trying to loosen his tense muscles by an act of will.

You're getting to where you jump at shadows. Much good you'll be to Ellemir, unless you can get your nerves in order.

His gloved hand went to the chain about his neck; there, wrapped in silk inside a small pouch of leather, he could feel the hard shape, the curious warmth of the matrix he carried. Given to him when he had mastered its use, the "starstone" Reidel had spoken about, it was keyed to his mind in a way no one but a Darkovan — and Comyn-telepath could ever understand. Long training had taught him to amplify the magnetic forces of his brain with the curious crystalline structure of the stone; and now the very touch of it quieted his mind to calm; the long discipline of the highly trained telepath.

Reason, he told himself, *all things in order.* As the disquiet lessened, he felt the quiet pulse and slow euphoria which meant his brain had begun to function at what the Comyn called basic, or "resting," rhythm. From this moment of calm, above himself, he looked at his fears and Reidel's. Something here to be examined, yes; but not to be chewed over restlessly from confused tales as he rode. Rather, something to be set aside, thought about, then systematically investigated, with facts rather than fears, happenings rather than gossip.

A wild shout ripped into his mind, crashing his artificial calm like a stone flung through a glass window. It was a painful, shattering shock, and he cried aloud with the impact of fear and agony on his mind, half a moment before he heard a hoarse male scream — a fearful scream, a scream which comes only from dying lips. His horse plunged and reared upward beneath him; his hand still clutching the crystal at his throat, he hauled desperately at the reins, trying to get control of his pitching mount. The animal stopped short under him, standing stiff-legged and trembling, as Damon stared in amazement, watching Reidel slide slowly to the ground, limp and unmistakably dead, his throat a single long gash, from which blood still spouted in a crimson fountain.

And no one was near him! A sword from nowhere, an invisible claw of steel to rip out the throat of a living, breathing man.

31

"Aldones! Lord of Light deliver us!" Damon whispered to himself, clutching the hilt of his knife, struggling for self-control. The other Guardsmen were fighting, their swords sweeping in great gleaming arcs against them.

Damon clutched the crystal in his fingers, fighting a silent battle for mastery of this illusion —*for illusion it must be!* Slowly, as through a thick veil in his mind, he saw shadowy forms, strange and hardly human. The light seemed to shine *through* them, and his eyes went in and out of focus, trying hard to keep them before him.

And he was unarmed! No swordsman at best —

He gripped the reins of his horse, struggling against the impulse to rush in against the invisible opponents. Red fury pulsed in his blood, but an icy wave of reason told him, coldly, that he was unarmed, that he could only plunge in and die with his men, and that his duty to his kinswoman now came first. Was her house besieged by some such invisible terrors? Were they, perchance, lying in wait to keep any of her kinfolk from coming to her aid?

His men were fighting wildly against the invisible assailants; Damon, clutching the matrix, wheeled his mount and swerved, dashing away from the attackers at a hard gallop, and down the path. His throat seemed to crawl. For all he knew some invisible blade might sweep out of empty air and strike his head from his shoulders. Behind him the hoarse cries of his men were like a knife in his heart, clutching at him, clawing at his conscience. He rode, head down, cloak clutched about him, as if indeed demons pursued him; and he did not slacken pace until he came to a halt, his horse trembling and streaming sweat, his own breath coming in great ragged heaving gasps, on the next hill rise, two or three miles below the ambush, and above him the high gates of Armida.

Dismounting, he drew the crystal from its protective leather pouch and unwrapped the silk within. *Naked, this could have saved us all,* he thought, looking down despairingly at the blue stone with the strange, curling gleams of fire within; his trained telepathic power, enormously amplified by the resonating magnetic fields of the matrix, could have mastered the illusion; his men might have had to fight, but they would have fought free of illusions, against foes they could see, who could match them fairly. He bowed his head. A matrix was never carried bare; its resonating vibrations had to be insulated from what was around it. And by the time he could have freed it from its insulation, his men would have been dead, anyway, and him with them.

Sighing, and thrusting the crystal back into the silk, he patted his exhausted horse on the flank, and, not mounting to spare the gasping, trembling beast any further exertion, he led him slowly up the rise toward the gates. Armida was not besieged, it seemed. The courtyard lay quiet and bare in the dying sunlight, and the nightly fog was beginning to roll in from the surrounding hills; serving men came to take his horse and cried out in alarm at the state of it.

"Were you pursued? Lord Damon, where is your escort?"

He shook his head slowly, not trying to answer. "Later, later. Tend my horse, and let him not drink until he is cooled; he has ridden too far at a gallop. Send for the Lady Ellemir to tell her I have come."

If this mission is not of grave importance, he said to himself grimly, *we shall quarrel. Four of my faithful men dead, and horribly. Yet she is under no siege or trouble.*

Then he became aware of the grim quiet that lay over the courtyard. Surely there were splotches of blood on the stones. A strange disquiet, a sickening unease — which he knew was in his mind, sensed from something not on this mundane level at all — crept slowly over him.

He raised his eyes to see Ellemir Lanart standing before him.

"Kinsman," she said half audibly. "I heard something — not enough to be sure. I thought it was you, too —" Her voice failed, and she threw herself into his arms.

"Damon! Damon! I thought you were dead, too!"

Damon Ridenow held the girl gently, stroking the shaking shoulders. Her bright head dropped heavily for a moment against him, and she sighed, then, fighting for control, raised her head. She was very tall and slender, her fire-red hair proclaiming her a member of Damon's own telepath caste; her features were delicate, her eyes brilliant blue.

"Ellemir, what has happened here?" he asked, his apprehension growing. "Are you under attack? Has there been a raid?"

She lowered her head. "I do not know," she said. "All I know is that Callista is gone."

"Gone? In God's name what do you mean? Carried off by bandits? Run away? Eloped?" Even as he spoke he knew that was madness; Ellemir's twin sister Callista was a Keeper, one of those women trained to handle all the power of a circle of skilled telepaths; they were vowed to virginity, and surrounded with a circle of awe which meant no sane man on Darkover would raise his eyes to one. "Ellemir, tell me! I thought her safe in the Tower at Arilinn. Where? How?"

Ellemir was fighting for self-control. "We cannot talk here on the doorstep," she said, withdrawing from him and regaining her self-possession. Damon felt a moment of regret — her head against his shoulder had seemed to belong there somehow. He told himself incredulously that this was neither the time nor the place for such thoughts, and resisted the impulse to touch her hand lightly again, following her at a sedate pace into the great hall. But she was barely inside before she turned to him.

"She was here for a visit," Ellemir said in a shaking voice. "The Lady Leonie has sought to

35

lay down her Keeper's place and return to her home at Valeron, and Callista was to take her place in the Tower; but she came for a visit to me first, and she wished to persuade me to come to Arilinn and stay there with her, that she might not be so terribly alone. In any case, to see me for a little before she must be isolated for the making of the Tower Circle. All went well, although she seemed uneasy. I am no trained telepath, Damon, but Callista and I were twin-born and our minds can touch, a little, whether we will it or not. So I sensed her unease, but she said only that she had evil dreams of cat-hags and withering gardens and dying flowers. And then one day —" Ellemir's face paled and, hardly knowing what she did, she reached her hand to Damon's, gripping desperately as if to lean her weight upon him.

"I woke, hearing her scream; but no one else had heard any sound, even a whisper. Four of our people lay dead in the court, and among them — among them was our old foster mother Bethiah. She had nursed Callista at her breasts as a babe and she slept always on a cot at her feet, and she lay there with her eyes — her eyes clawed out of their sockets, still just alive." Ellemir was sobbing aloud now. "And Callista was gone! Gone, and I could not reach her — I could not reach her even with my mind! My twin, and she was gone, as if Avarra had snatched her alive into some otherworld."

Damon's voice was hard; he kept it that way

with a fierce effort. "Do you think she is dead, Ellemir?"

Ellemir met his eyes with a level blue gaze.

"I do not. I did not feel her die; and my twin could not die without my sharing her death. When our brother Coryn died in a fall from the aerie, taking hawks, both Callista and I felt him pass from life into death; and Callista is *my twin*. She lives." Then Ellemir's voice broke and she wept wildly.

"But where? Where? She is gone, gone, gone as if she had never lived! And only shadows moving since then — only shadows. Damon, Damon, what shall I do, what shall I do?"

Chapter
THREE

He would never have thought that going downhill could be so difficult.

All day Andrew Carr had climbed, scrambled, and slid around on the sharp rocks of the slope. He had looked down into an incredibly deep ravine where the remnants of the mapping plane lay smashed, and written off any lingering hope of salvaging food, protective clothing, or the identity disks of his companions. Now, as darkness fell and a light fall of snow began to drift across the slopes, he huddled inside the thick fur coat and sucked the last few of the sweets he had with him. He scanned the horizon below him for lights or any other signs of life. There must be some. This was a thickly inhabited planet. But out in the mountains here, it might be miles or even hundreds of miles between settled areas. He did see pale gleams against the horizon, one clustered group of lights which might even have been a town or village. So his only problem was to get down to it. But that might take some doing. He knew nothing — less than nothing, really — of woodcraft or survival skills. Finally, remembering something he had read, he half buried himself in a heap of dead leaves and pulled the flap of the fur coat over his head. He wasn't warm, and he found his thoughts dwelling lovingly on food, great steaming platefuls of it, but finally he did sleep; after a fashion, waking almost hourly to shiver and pull himself more deeply into his heap of leaves, but he did sleep. Nor did he see, anywhere in his confused dreams, the face of the ghostly girl he identified with his vision.

All the next day, and the day after, he struggled his way through, and down, a long slope covered with dense thorny underbrush, twice lost his way in the thickly wooded valley at the bottom, and finally toiled his way up the far side of the slope. From the bottom of the valley he had no way to ascertain which way he should be going, and from there, he saw no sign of human or other habitation. Once he came across remnants, in extreme disrepair, of a split-rail fence, and wasted a couple of hours walking its length — the existence of a fence usually postulated something to be fenced in, or kept out. But it led him only into thick, tangled dry vines and he decided that whatever strange kind of livestock had been fenced in at one time, both the stock and their keeper had been long, long gone. Near the spot where he had first found the fence was a dry creek bed, and he surmised that he could probably follow it down out of the mountains. Civilizations, especially farmlands, had always built their settlements along watercourses, and he believed that this planet would hardly be an exception. If he followed the stream down along its natural course, it would certainly lead him out of the hills and probably to the abodes of whatever people had built the fence and herded the stock. But after a few miles the course of the dry stream bed was obscured by a rock slide, and try as he might, he could not find it on the other side. Maybe that was why the fence-builders had moved their livestock.

Toward the end of the second day he found a few withered fruits clinging to a gnarled tree. They looked and tasted like apples, dry and hard but edible; he ate most of them and gathered the last few to be eaten later. He felt miserably frustrated. Probably there were other edibles all around him, everything from the bark of certain trees to the mushrooms or fungi he found growing on fallen wood. The trouble was that he couldn't tell the wholesome food plants from the deadly poisonous ones, and therefore he was only tantalizing himself by thinking about it.

Late that night, as he was searching for a windbreak in which to sleep, snow began to fall again, with a strange and persistent steadiness that made him uneasy. He had heard about the blizzards of the hills, and the thought of being caught out in one, without food or protective clothing or shelter, scared him out of his wits. Before long the snow became so heavy that he could hardly see his hand before his face, and his shoes were wet through and caked with the cold and gluey mass.

I'm finished, he thought grimly. *I was finished when the plane crashed, only I didn't have the sense to know it.*

The only chance I had — the only chance I ever had — was good weather, and now that's broken.

The only thing that made sense now was to pick out a comfortable place, preferably out of the damned wind that howled like a lost thing around the rocky crags above him, lie down, make himself comfortable, and fall asleep in the snow. That would be the end of it all. Considering how deserted this part of the world looked, it was likely to be so many years before anyone stumbled over his body, that no one would be able to tell whether he was a Terran or a native of this planet.

Damn that wind! It howled like a dozen wind machines, like a chorus of lost souls out of Dante's *Inferno.* There was a curious illusion in the wind. It sounded as if, very far away, someone was calling his name.

Andrew Carr! Andrew Carr!

It was an illusion, of course. No one within three hundred miles of this place even knew he was here, except maybe the ghostly girl he had seen when the plane crashed. If she *was* actually within three hundred miles of this place. And of course he had no idea if she actually knew his name, or not. Damn the girl, anyway, if she even existed. Which he doubted.

Carr stumbled and fell full length into the deepening snow. He started to rise, then thought, *Oh, hell, what's the use,* and let himself fall forward again.

Someone *was* calling his name.

Andrew Carr! Come this way, quickly! I can show you the way to shelter, but more I cannot do. You must take your own way there.

He heard himself say fretfully, against the dim voice that was like an echo inside his mind, "No. I'm too tired. I can't go any farther."

"Carr! Raise your eyes and look at me!"

Resentfully, shielding his eyes against the howling wind and the sharp needles of the snow, Andrew Carr braced himself with his palms and looked up. He already knew what he would see.

It was the girl, of course.

She wasn't really there. How could she be there, wearing a thin blue gown that looked like a torn nightdress, barefoot, her hair not even blowing in the bitter snow-laden wind?

He heard himself say aloud — and heard the words ripped by the wind from his mouth and carried away, so that the girl could not possibly have heard them from ten feet away, "What are you doing now? Are you really here? Where are you?"

She said precisely, in that low-pitched voice which seemed always to carry just to his ear and not an inch farther, "I do not know where I am, or I would not be there, since it is nowhere I wish to be. The important thing is that I know where you are, and where the only place of safety is for you. Follow me, quickly! Get up, you fool, get up!"

Carr stumbled to his feet, clutching his coat about him. She stood, it seemed, about eight feet ahead of him in the storm. She was still clad in the flimsy and torn nightdress, but although her bare feet and shoulders gleamed palely through the rents in the garment, she did not seem to be shivering at all.

She beckoned — now that she knew she had his attention, it seemed, she would not waste any more effort trying to make herself heard — and began to walk lightly across the snow. Her feet, he noticed with a weird sense of unreality, were not quite touching the ground. *Yeah, that figures, if she's a ghost.*

Head down, he stumbled after the retreating figure of the girl. The wind tore at his coat, sent it flapping out wildly behind him. His shoes were thick, half-frozen lumps of wet snow, and his hair and the stubble of beard were icy streaks of roughness against his face. Now that the snow had obscured the ground to even whiteness, covering the lumps and shadows, two or three times he tripped over some hidden root or unseen chuckhole, and measured his length on the ground; but each time he struggled up and followed the shadow ahead of him. She had saved his life once before. *She must know what she's doing.*

It seemed a very long time that he floundered

and stumbled in the snow, although he thought afterward that it was probably not more than three-quarters of an hour, before he blundered full into what felt like a brick wall. He put out his hand, incredulous.

It *was* a brick wall. Or, anyway, it felt like one. It felt like the side of a building, and feeling about a little, he found a door which was made of planed wood, worn smooth, and fastened with stiff leather straps, hauled through a rough-cut wooden latch, and knotted. It took him some time to tease the wet leather knot apart, and he finally had to take off his gloves and fumble with stiff bare fingers which were blue and bleeding by the time the knot finally yielded. The door creaked open and Carr cautiously stepped inside. For all he knew he might have found light, fire, and people sitting around a supper table; but the place was dark and cold and deserted. But not half as cold as the outdoors, and at least it was dry. There was something like straw on the floor, and the dim light of reflected snow from outside showed him vague shapes that might have been cattle stanchions, or furniture. He had no way of making a light, but it was so quiet that he knew neither the animals which had once been stabled here, nor their keepers, still inhabited the place.

Once again the girl had led him to safety. He sank down on the mercifully dry floor, scooped a comfortable place in the straw, took off his sopping wet shoes, dried his chilled and numb feet on the straw, and lay down to sleep. He looked around for the ghostly form of the girl who had guided him here, but as he had expected, she was gone.

He woke, hours later, out of the deep sleep of exhaustion, to a raging snow-whitened world, a howling inferno of blowing sleet and ice battering against the building where he lay. But enough light filtered through the heavily fastened wooden shutters so that he could see the inside of the building where he lay: empty except for the thick straw and the uprights of stanchions. It smelled, very faintly, of long-dried animal dung, a sharp but not unpleasant pungency.

In the far corner was a dark mass of something, which he curiously explored. He found a few rags of strangely fashioned clothing. One, a warm, blanketlike cloak of ragged and faded tartan cloth, he took to wrap himself in. Under the heaped clothing — which was ragged but, because of the dryness of the building, untouched by mold or mildew — he found a heavy chest fastened shut with a hasp, but not locked. Opening it, he discovered food; forgotten, or most likely left over for another herding season by the keepers of whatever strange beasts had once been kept here. There was a form of dried bread — actually more like hardtack or crackers — wrapped in oiled paper. There was some leathery unrecognizable stuff which he finally decided must be dried meat; but neither his teeth nor his palate could cope with it. Some pasty, fragrant stuff reminded him of peanut

45

butter, and it went well on the hardtack, made of crushed seeds or nuts with dried fruit mashed up in it. There was some kind of dried fruit, but it, too, was so hard that, although it smelled good, he decided it would need a good long soak in water, preferably hot water, before approaching anything like edibility.

He satisfied his hunger with the hardtack and the nut-and-fruit-butter paste, and after hunting around, discovered a crude water tap that ran into a basin, apparently for watering the beasts. He drank, and splashed a little cold water on his face. It was far too cold for any more meticulous washing, but he felt better even for that much. Then, wrapped in the tartan blanket, he explored the place end to end. He was much relieved when he found the final convenience, a crude earth-closet latrine roughly enclosed at the far end. He had not relished the thought of either venturing out into the storm, even for a moment, or of defiling the place against the possible future return of its owners. It crossed his mind that the conveniences, and the stored provisions, must have been provided against just such blizzards as this, when neither man nor beast could live without some shelter.

So this world was not only inhabited, it was civilized, at least after a fashion. *All the comforts of home,* he thought, returning to his bed of piled straw. Now all he had to do was to wait out the blizzard.

He was so weary, after days of climbing and

walking, and so warm in the thick blanket, that he had no trouble at all in falling asleep again. When he woke again, the light was declining, and the noise of the storm was lessening a little. He guessed, by the gathering darkness, that he had slept most of the day away.

And it's early fall. What must it be like here in the winter? This planet might make a great winter-sports resort, but it's not fit for anything else. I pity the people who live here!

He made another meager meal of hard crackers and fruit-and-nut paste (good enough, but boring for a regular diet), and because it was too cold and dark to do anything else, he wrapped himself up again, and stretched out in the straw.

He had slept his fill, and he was no longer cold, nor very hungry. It was too dark to see much, but there was not a great deal to see in any case. He thought randomly, *Too bad I'm not a trained xenologist. No Terran has ever been let loose on this world before.* He knew there were skilled sociologists and anthropologists who, with the artifacts he had seen (and eaten), could skillfully analyze the exact level of this planet's culture, or at least of those people who lived in this area. The sturdy brick or stone walls, squarely mortared together, the cattle stanchions constructed of wood and nailed together with wooden pegs, the water tap of hardwood which ran into a stone basin, the unglazed windows covered only with tight wooden shutters, said one thing about the culture: it went with the fence rails and the rude earth-closet latrine, a low-level agricultural society. Yet he wasn't sure. This was, after all, a herdsman's shelter, a bad-weather retreat for emergencies, and no civilization wasted much technical accomplishment on them. There was also the kind of sophisticated foresight which built such things at all, and stocked them with imperishable food, against need, even guarding against the need to go out momentarily for calls of nature. The blanket was beautifully woven, with a craftsmanship rare in these days of synthetics and disposable fabrics. And so he realized that the people of this planet might be far more civilized than he thought.

He shifted his weight on the crackling straw, and blinked, for the girl was there again in the darkness. She was still wearing the torn, thin blue dress that gleamed with a pale, icelike glitter in the dimness of the dark barn. For a moment, even though he still half believed that she was a hallucination, he could not help saying aloud, "Aren't you cold?"

It is not cold where I am.

This, Carr told himself, was absolutely freaky. He said slowly, "Then you're not here?"

How could I be where you are? If you think I am there — no, here — try to touch me.

Hesitantly, Carr stretched out his hand. It seemed that he must touch her bare round arm, but there was nothing palpable to the touch. He said doggedly, "I don't understand any of this. You're here, and you're not here. I can see you, and you're a ghost. You say your name is Callista, but that's a name from my own world. I still think I'm crazy, and I'm talking to myself, but I'd love to know how you can explain any of this."

The ghost-girl made a sound that was like soft childlike laughter. "I do not understand it either," she said quietly. "As I tried to tell you before, it was not you I attempted to reach but my kinswoman and my friends. But wherever I search, they are not there. It is as if their minds had been wiped off this world. For a long time I wandered around in dark places, until I found myself looking into your eyes. It seemed that I knew you, even though my eyes had never looked on you before. And then, something in you kept drawing me back. Somewhere, not in this world at all, we have touched one another. I am nothing to you, but I had brought you into danger, so I sought to save you. And I come back because" — for a moment it seemed that she was about to weep — "I am very much alone, and even a stranger is better than no companion. Do you want me to go away again?"

"No," Carr said quickly, "stay with me, Callista. But I don't understand this at all."

She was silent for a minute, as if considering. *God,* Carr thought, *how real she seems.* He could see her breathing, the faint rise and fall of her chest beneath the thin, torn dress. One of her feet was smudged: no, bruised and reddened and

49

bloodstained. Carr said, "Are you hurt?"

"Not really. You asked me how I could be there with you. I suppose you know that we live in more than one way, and that the world you are in now is the solid world, the world of *things,* the world of hard bodies and physical creations. But in the world where I am, we leave our bodies behind like outgrown clothing or cast snakeskins, and what we call *place* has no real being. I am used to that world, I have been trained to walk in it, but somehow I am being kept in a part of it where no other of my people's minds may touch. As I wandered in that gray and featureless plain, your thoughts touched mine and I felt you clearly, like hand clasping hand in the darkness."

"Are you in darkness?"

"Where my body is being kept, I am in darkness, yes. But in the gray world, I can see you, even as you can see me. That is how I saw your flying machine crash and knew it would fall into the ravine. And I saw you lost in the snowstorm and I knew you were near to this herdsman's hut. I came here now to show you where food was kept if you had not found it."

"I found it," Carr said. "I don't know what to say. I thought you were a dream and you're acting as if you were real."

It sounded again like soft laughter. "Oh, I assure you, I am just as real and solid as you are yourself. And I would give a great deal to be with you in that cold, dark herdsman's hut, since it is only a few miles from my home, and as soon as

50

the storm subsides I could be free and by my own fireside. But I —"

In the middle of a word, she was abruptly gone, winked out like a breath. For some strange reason this did more to convince Carr of her reality than anything she had said. If he'd been imagining her, if his subconscious mind had hallucinated her, as men cold and alone and in danger *did* hallucinate strangers from their deepest wishes, he'd have kept her there; he'd at least have let her finish what she was saying. The fact that she'd vanished in the middle of a phrase tended to indicate not only that she had really been there, in some intangible sense, but that some unknown third party had a superior power over her comings and goings.

She was frightened, and she was sad. *I am very much alone, and even a stranger is better than no companion.*

Cold and alone on a strange and unfamiliar world, Andrew Carr could understand that very well. It was just about the way he felt himself.

Not that she'd be all that bad as a companion, if she were really here. . . .

Not a great deal of satisfaction out of a companion you can't touch. And yet . . . even though he couldn't lay a hand on her, there was something surprisingly compelling about the girl.

He'd known lots of women, at least in the Biblical sense. Known their bodies and a little about their personalities, and what they wanted out of life. But he'd never got close enough to any one of them that he felt bad when the time came for them to go off in opposite directions.

Let's face it. From the minute I saw this girl in the crystal, she's been so real to me that I was willing to turn my whole life around, just on the off chance that she was something more than a dream. And now I know she's real. She's saved my life once: no, twice. I wouldn't have lasted long out in that blizzard. And she's in trouble. They're keeping her in the dark, she says, and she doesn't even know for sure where she is.

If I come out of this alive, I'm going to find her, if it takes me the rest of my life. Lying wrapped in his fur coat and blanket, in a musty heap of straw, alone on a strange world, Carr suddenly realized that the change in his life, the change that had begun when he saw the girl in the crystal and had thrown over his job and his life to stay on her world, was complete. He had found his new direction, and it led toward the girl. *His* girl. His woman, now and for the rest of his life. Callista.

He was cynic enough to jeer a little at himself. Yeah. He didn't know where she was, who she was, or what she was; she might be married with six children (well, hardly, at her age); she might be a ghastly bitch — who knew what women were like on this world? All he knew about her was . . .

All he knew about her was that in some way she'd touched him, come closer to him than anyone had ever come before. He knew that she was lonely and miserable and frightened, that she couldn't get in touch with her own people, that for some reason she needed him. All he knew about her was all he needed to know about her: she needed him. For some reason he was all she had to cling to, and if she wanted his life she could have it. He'd hunt her up somehow, get her away from whoever was keeping her in the dark, hurting her, and frightening her. He'd get her free. (*Yeah,* sneered his cynical other self, *quite the hero, slaying dragons for your fair lady,* but he turned the jeer off harshly.) And after that, when she was free and happy —

After that, well, we'll cross that bridge when we come to it, he said firmly, and curled down to sleep again.

The storm lasted, as nearly as he could tell (his chronometer had evidently been damaged in the crash and never ran again), for five days. On the third or fourth of those days he woke in dim light to see the girl's shadowy form, stilled, sleeping, close beside him; still disoriented, rousing to sharp, intense physical awareness of her — round, lovely, clad only in the flimsy, torn thin garment which seemed to be all she was wearing — he reached out to draw her close into his arms; then, with the sharp shock of disappointment, he realized there was nothing to touch. As if the very intensity of his thoughts had reached her, awareness flashed over her sleeping face and the large gray eyes opened; she looked at him in surprise and faint dismay.

"I am sorry," she murmured. "You — startled me."

Carr shook his head, trying to orient himself. "I'm the one to be sorry," he said. "I guess I must have thought I was dreaming and it didn't matter. I didn't mean to offend you."

"I'm not offended," she said simply, looking straight into his eyes. "If I were here beside you like this, you would have every right to expect — I only meant, I am sorry to have unwittingly aroused a desire I cannot satisfy. I did not do it willingly. I must have been thinking of you in my sleep, stranger. I cannot go on simply thinking of you as *stranger*," Callista said, a flicker of faint amusement passing over her face.

"My name's Andrew Carr," he said, and felt her soft repetition of the name.

"Andrew. I am sorry, Andrew. I must have been thinking of you in my sleep and so drawn to you without waking." With no further sign of haste or fluster, she drew her clothes more carefully around her bare breasts and smoothed the diaphanous folds of her skirt down around her round thighs. She smiled and now there was a glimmer almost of mischief in her sad face. "Ah, this is sad! The first time, the very first, that I lie down with any man, and I am not able to enjoy it! But it's naughty of me to tease you. Please don't think I am so badly brought up as all that."

Deeply touched, as much by her brave attempt to make a joke as anything else, Andrew said gently, "I couldn't think anything of you that wasn't good, Callista. I only wish" — and to his own surprise he felt his voice breaking — "I wish

54

there was some real comfort I could give you."

She reached out her hand — almost as if, Andrew thought in surprise, she too had forgotten for a moment that he was not physically present to her — and laid it over his wrist. He could see his own wrist through the delicate appearance of her fingers, but the illusion was somehow very comforting, anyhow. She said, "I suppose it is something, that you can give companionship and" — her voice wavered; she was crying — "and the sense of a human presence to someone who is alone in the dark."

He watched her weep, torn apart by the sight of her tears. When she had collected herself a little, he asked, "Where are you? Can I help you somehow?"

She shook her head. "As I told you. They have kept me in the dark, since if I knew exactly where I was, I could be elsewhere. Since I do not know precisely, I can leave this place only in my spirit; my body must perforce stay where they have confined it, and they must know that. *Curse them!*"

"Who are *they*, Callista?"

"I don't know that, exactly, either," she said, "but I suspect they are not men, since they have offered me no physical harm except blows and kicks. It is the only thing for which a woman of the Domains may be grateful when she is in the hands of the other folk — at least with them she need not fear ravishment. For the first several days in their hands, I spent night and day in

55

hourly terror of rape; when it did not come, I knew I was not in human hands. Any man in these mountains would know how to make me powerless to fight them . . . whereas the other folk have no recourse except to take away my jewels, lest one of them should be a starstone, and to keep me in darkness so I can do them no harm with the light of sun or stars."

Andrew didn't understand any of that. Not in human hands? Then who were her captors? He asked another question.

"If you are in the dark, how can you see me?"

"I see you in the overlight," she said quietly, telling him nothing at all. "As you see me. Not the light of this world — look. You know, I suppose, that the things we call solid are only appearances, tiny particles of energy strung together and whirling wildly around, with much more of empty space than of solidness."

"Yes, I know that." It was an odd way to explain molecular and atomic energy, but it got her meaning across.

"Well, then. Strung to your solid body by these energy webs there are other bodies, and if you are taught, you can use them in the world of that level. How can I say this? Of the level of solidness where you are. Your solid body walks on this world, this solid planet under your solid feet, and you need the solid light of our sun. It is powered by your mind, which moves your solid brain, and the solid brain sends messages that move your arms and legs and so forth. Your mind also powers your lighter bodies, each one with its own electric nerve-net of energy. In the world of the overlight, where we are now, there is no such thing as darkness, because the light does not come from a solid sun. It comes from the energy-net body of the sun, which can shine — how can I say this? — right through the energy-net body of the planet. The solid body of the planet can shut out the light of the solid sun, but not the energy-net light. Is that clear?"

"I suppose so," he said slowly, trying to cope with it. It sounded like the old story of astral duplicates of the body and astral planes, in her own language, which he supposed was reaching his mind directly from hers. "The important thing is that you can come here. There have been times when I've wanted to step out and leave my body behind."

"Oh, you do," she said literally. "Everyone does in sleep, when the energy-nets fall apart. But you have not been trained to do it at will. Someday, perhaps, I can teach you how it is done." She laughed a little ruefully. "If we both live, that is. If we both live."

Chapter
FOUR

Outside the thick walls of the great house at Armida, the white blizzard raged, howling and whining around the heights as if animated by a personal fury against the stone walls which kept it at bay. Even inside, in the great hall, the windows were grayed with its blur and the wind reached them as a dulled roar. Restless and distraught, Ellemir paced the length of the hall. With a nervous glance at the raging storm outside, she said, "We cannot even search for her in this weather! And with every hour that passes, it may be that she is farther and farther away." She turned on Damon like a fury, and demanded, "How can you sit there so calmly, toasting your toes, when Callista is somewhere in this storm?"

Damon raised his head and said quietly, "Come and sit down, Ellemir. We may be reasonably sure that wherever Callista may be, she is not out in the snowstorm. Whoever went to so much trouble to steal her from here did not do it to let her die of exposure in the hills. As for searching for her, were the weather never so good, we could not go out and quarter the

Kilghard Hills on horseback, shouting her name in the forests." He had spoken with wry humor, but Ellemir whirled on him angrily.

"Are you saying we can do nothing, that we are helpless, that we must abandon her to whatever fate has seized her?"

"I am saying nothing of the sort," Damon told her. "You heard what I said. We could not search for her at random in these hills, even if the weather would allow it. If she were in any ordinary hiding place, you could touch her mind. Let us use these days of the storm to begin the search in some reasonable way, and the best way to do that is to sit down, and think about it. Do come and sit down, Ellemir," he pleaded. "Pacing the floor, and tearing your nerves to shreds, will not help Callista. It will only make you less fit to help her when the time comes. You have not eaten; you look as if you have not slept. Come, kinswoman. Sit here by the fire. Let me give you some wine." He rose and led the girl to a seat. She looked up with her lips trembling and said, "Don't be kind to me, Damon, or I'll break down and melt."

"It might do you good if you could," he said, pouring her a glass of wine. She sipped it slowly, and he stood by the fireplace, looking down at her. He said, "I have been thinking. You told me Callista complained of evil dreams — withering gardens, cat-hags?"

"That is so."

Damon nodded. He said, "I rode from Serrais with a party of Guards, and Reidel — a Guardsman of my company — spoke of misfortune that had fallen on his kinsman. He was said to have raved — listen to this — of the darkening lands, and of great fires and winds that brought death, and girls who clawed at his soul like cat-hags. From many men, I would have dismissed this as mere babble, imagination. But I have known Reidel all my life. He does not babble, and as far as I have ever been able to determine, he has no more imagination than one of his own saddle-bags. *Had,* I should say; the poor fellow is dead. But he was speaking of what he had seen and heard, and I think it more than coincidence. And I told you of the ambush, when we were struck by invisible attackers with invisible swords and weapons. This alone would tell me that something very strange is going on in the heights they have begun to call the darkening lands. Since it is rather less than unlikely that there would be two complete sets of bizarre happenings in one part of the country, it makes sense to begin with the assumption that what happened to my Guardsmen is somehow associated with what happened to Callista."

"That seems likely," she said. "This tells me something else. It was no human being who tore out old Bethiah's eyes as she fought to save her fosterling." She shuddered, wrapping her arms around her shoulders as if she were icy cold. "Damon! It is possible, can it be, that Callista is in the hands of the cat-people?"

"It seems not impossible," Damon said.

60

"But what could they want with her? What will they do with her? What — what —"

"How should I know, Ellemir? I could only guess. I know so little of those folk, even though I fought them. I have never seen one of them, except lying as a corpse on a battlefield. There are those who believe that they are as intelligent as mankind, and there are those who believe they are little more than brutes. I do not think that anyone since the days of Varzil the Good really knows anything about them for certain."

"No, there is one thing we know for certain," Ellemir said grimly, "that they fight like men, and sometimes even more fiercely."

"That, yes," said Damon, and was silent, thinking of his Guard, ambushed and lying dead on the hillsides below Armida. They had died so that he could sit here by the fireside with Ellemir. He knew he could have done nothing to save them, and sharing their death would have done no good to anyone, but all the same guilt tore at him and would not be eased. "When the storm subsides I must make shift somehow to go back and bury them," he said, adding after a moment, "If there is enough left of them to bury."

Ellemir said, quoting a well-known mountain proverb, "The dead in heaven is too happy to grieve for indignities to his corpse; the dead in hell has too much else to grieve for."

"Still," said Damon stubbornly, "for the sake of their kinsfolk, I would do what I can."

"It is Callista's fate that troubles me now,"

61

Ellemir said. "Damon! Can you possibly be serious? Can you really believe that Callista is in the hands of nonhumans? Beyond all other considerations, what could they possibly *want* with her?"

"As for that, child, I know no more than you do," said Damon. "It is just possible — and we must accept the possibility — that they stole her for some unexplainable reason, comprehensible only to nonhumans, which we, being human, can never know or comprehend."

"That is no help at all!" Ellemir said angrily. "It sounds like the horror tales I heard in the nursery! So-and-so was stolen by monsters, and when I asked why the monsters stole her, Nurse told me that it was because they were monsters, and monsters were evil —" She broke off and her voice caught again. "This is *real,* Damon! She's my *sister!* Don't tell me fairy stories!"

Damon looked at her levelly. "Nothing was further from my mind. I told you before; no one *really* knows anything about the cat-folk."

"Except that they are evil!"

"What is evil?" Damon asked wearily. "Say they do evil to our own people, and I will agree heartily with you. But if you say that they are evil in themselves, for no reason and just for the pleasure of doing evil, then you are making them into those fairy-story monsters you're talking about. I only said that since we are human and they are cat-people, we may have to accept that we may not be able to understand, now or ever, what their reasons for taking her may have been. But that is simply something to keep in mind — that any reasons we might guess for her kidnapping may simply be human approximations of *their* reasons, and not the whole truth. Apart from that, though, why do any folk steal women, and why Callista in particular? Or, for that matter, any beasts steal? I have never heard that they were cannibal flesh-eaters, and in any case the forests are filled with game at this season, so we may assume it was not that."

"Are you trying to give me the horrors?" Ellemir still sounded angry.

"Not a bit of it. I'm trying to do *away* with the horrors," Damon said. "If there was any vague thought in your mind that she might have been killed and eaten, I think you can dismiss it. Since they killed her guards, and disabled her foster mother, it was not just *any* human being they wanted, or even any woman. So they took her, not because she was human, not just because she was female, but because she was one specific female human: because she was Callista."

Ellemir said, low, "Bandits and trail-raiders steal young women, at times, for slaves, or concubines, or to sell in the Dry Towns —"

"I think we can forget that too," said Damon firmly. "They left all your serving-girls; in any case, what would cat-men want with a human female? There are stories of crossbreeds between man and *chieri,* back in the ancient times, but even those are mostly legends and no man living

63

can say whether or not they have any foundation in fact. As for the other folk, our women are no more to them than theirs to us. Of course, it is possible that they have some human captive who wanted a wife, but even if they were so altruistic and kind as to be willing to provide him with one, which I admit I find hard to believe, there were a dozen serving-girls in the outbuildings, as young as Callista, just as beautiful, and infinitely easier to come at. If they simply wanted human women, as hostages, or to sell somewhere as slaves, they would have taken them as well. Or taken them, and left Callista."

"Or me. Why take Callista from her bed and leave me sleeping untouched in mine?"

"That, too. You and Callista are twins. *I* can tell you one from the other, but I have known you since your hair was too short to braid. A casual stranger could never have known you apart, and might easily have taken Callista for you. Now it's barely possible that they were simply wanting a hostage, or someone to hold to ransom, and snatched the one who came first to hand."

"No," Ellemir said, "my bed is nearest the door, and they walked very quietly and carefully around me to come at her."

"Then it comes to the one difference between you," Damon told her. "Callista is a telepath and a Keeper. You are not. We can only assume that in some way they knew which of you was the telepath, and that for some reason they wanted specifically to take the one woman here who fitted that description. Why? I know no more than you do, but I am sure that was their reason."

"And all this still leaves us no nearer to a solution," Ellemir said, and she sounded frantic. "The facts are that she is gone, and we don't know where she is! So all your talk is no good at all!"

"No? Think a little," said Damon. "We know she has probably not been killed, except by accident; if they went to such great pains to take her, they will probably treat her with great care, feed her well, keep her warm, cherish her as a prize. She may be frightened and lonely, but she is probably neither cold, hungry, nor in pain, and it is very unlikely that she has suffered physical abuse or molestation. Also, it is quite probable that she has not been raped. That, at least, should ease your mind."

Ellemir raised the forgotten wine glass and sipped at it. She said, "But it doesn't help us get her back, or even know where to look." Just the same, she sounded calmer, and Damon was glad.

He said, "One thing at a time, girl. Perhaps, after the storm —"

"After the storm, whatever tracks or traces they might have left would be blotted out," Ellemir said.

"From all I hear, the cat-folk leave no tracks a man could read; hardly traces for another cat. In any case, I'm no tracker," Damon said. "If I can help you at all, that won't be the way."

Her eyes widened and suddenly she clutched at his arm.

"Damon! You're a telepath too, you've had some training — can you find Callista that way?"

She looked so excited, so happy and alive at the prospect, that it crushed Damon to have to smash that hope, but he knew he must. He said, "It isn't that easy, Ellemir. If you, her twin, can't reach her mind, there must be some reason."

"But I've had no training, I know so little," Ellemir said hopefully, "and you were Tower-trained —"

The man sighed. "That's true. And I'll try," he said. "I always meant to try. But don't hope for too much, *breda*."

"Will you try *now?*" she pleaded.

"I'll do what I can. First, bring me something of Callista's — jewelry she wears a good deal, a garment she has often worn, something of that sort."

While Ellemir went to fetch it, Damon drew his starstone from the protective silk wrappings about it, and gazed at it, broodingly. Telepath, yes, and Tower-trained in the old telepath sciences of Darkover — for a little while. And the hereditary Gift, the *laran* or telepathic power of the Ridenow family, was the psychic sensing of extrahuman forces, bred into the genetic material of the Ridenow Domain for just such work as this, centuries ago. But in these latter days, the old Darkovan noncausal sciences had fallen into disuse; because of intermarriage, inbreeding, the ancient *laran* Gifts rarely bred true. Damon had inherited his own family Gift in full measure, but all his life he had found it a curse, not a blessing, and he shied away from using it now.

As he had shied away from using it — he faced the fact squarely now, and his own guilt — to save his men. He had sensed danger. The trip which should have been peaceful, routine, a family mission, had turned into a nightmare, reeking with the feel of danger. Yet he had not had the courage to use his starstone, the matrix stone given him during his Tower training, and too intimately keyed to the telepath patterns of his mind to be used or even touched by anyone else.

Because he feared it . . . he had always feared it.

Time reeled, slid momentarily away, annihilating fifteen years that lay between, and a younger Damon stood, with bowed head, before the Keeper Leonie, that same Leonie now aging, whose place Callista was to have taken. Not a young woman even then, Leonie, and far from beautiful, her flame-colored hair already fading, her body flat and spare, but her gray eyes gentle and compassionate.

"No, Damon. It is not that you have failed, or displeased me. And all of us — I myself — love you, and value you. But you are too sensitive, you cannot barricade yourself. Had you been born a woman, in a woman's body," she added, laying a light hand on his shoulder, "you would have been a Keeper, perhaps one of the greatest. But as a man" — faintly, she shrugged — "you would destroy yourself, tear yourself apart. Perhaps, free of the Tower, you may be able to surround yourself with other things, grow less sensitive, less" — she hesitated, groping for the exact word — "less vulnerable. It is for your own good that I send you away, Damon; for your health, for your happiness, perhaps for your very sanity." Lightly, almost a breath, her lips brushed his forehead. "You know I love you; for that reason I do not want to destroy you. Go, Damon."

From that there was no appeal, and Damon had gone, cursing the vulnerability, the Gift he carried like a curse.

He had made a new career for himself in Comyn Council, and although he was no soldier and no swordsman, had taken his turn at commanding the Guardsmen: driven, constantly needing to prove himself. He never admitted even to himself how deeply that hour with Leonie had torn at his manhood. From any work with the starstone (although he carried it still, since it had been made a part of him), he had shied away in horror and panic.

And now he must, though his mind, his nerves, all his senses, were screaming revolt. . . .

He jolted back to present time as Ellemir said tentatively, "Damon, are you asleep?"

He shook his head to clear it of the phantoms of past failure and fear. "No, no. Preparing myself. What have you for me of Callista's?"

She opened her hand; a silver filigree butterfly lay within, daintily starred with multicolored gemstones. "Callista always wore this in her

68

hair," Ellemir said, and indeed a strand or two of long, silken hair was still entangled in the clasp.

"You are sure it is hers? I suppose like all sisters you share your ornaments — my own sisters used to complain of that."

Ellemir turned to show him the butterfly-shaped clasp at the nape of her own neck. She said, "Father always had her ornaments fashioned in silver and mine in gilt, so that we could tell them apart. He had these made for us in Carthon years ago, and she has worn it in her hair every day since then. She does not care much for jewelry, so she gave me the bracelet to match it, but the clasp she always wears."

That sounded circumstantial and convincing. Damon took the silver clasp between his fingers, closing his eyes, tentatively trying to sense what he could from it. "Yes, this is Callista's," he said after a moment, and she said, "Can you really tell?"

Damon shrugged. "Give me yours for a moment," he said, and Ellemir turned and drew the matching clasp from her own hair, turning modestly aside so that he caught only the faintest glimpse of her bare neck. He was so sensitized to her at that moment that even that momentary and fleeting glimpse jerked a string of sensual awareness and response deep in his body; firmly he put it away on a deeper level of consciousness. No time for that now. Ellemir laid the gilded ornament in his hand. It tingled with the feel of her very self. Damon drew a deep breath and forced the awareness below conscious level again. He said, "Close your eyes."

Childishly, she screwed them up tight.

"Hold out your hands. . . ." Damon laid one of the ornaments in each small pink palm. "Now, if you cannot tell me which is your own, you are no child of the Alton Domain. . . ."

"I was tested for *laran* as a child," Ellemir protested, "and told I had none, compared with Callista —"

"Never compare yourself with anyone," Damon said, with a sudden rough thrust of anger. "Concentrate, Ellemir."

She said, with a queer strange note of surprise in her voice, "This is mine — I am sure."

"Look and see."

She opened her blue eyes, and gazed in astonishment at the gilt butterfly clasp in her hand. "Why, it is! The other one felt strange, this one — How did I do that?"

Damon shrugged. "This one — yours — has the impress of your personality, your vibrations, on it," he said. "It would have been simpler still if you and Callista were not twins, for twins share much in vibration. That was why I wanted to be quite, quite sure you had never worn hers, since it is difficult enough to tell twin from twin by their telepathic imprint alone. Of course, since Callista is a Keeper, her imprint is more definite." He broke off, feeling a sudden surge of anger. Ellemir had always lived in her twin's shadow. And she was too good, too gentle and good, to resent it. Why should she be so humble?

Forcibly, he calmed the irrational surge of rage. He said quietly, "I think you have more *laran* than you realize, although it is true that, in twins, one seems always to get more than her fair share of the Gift, and the other rather less. This is why the best Keepers are often one of a twin-pair, since she has her own and a part of her sister's share of the psi potentials."

He cupped the starstone between his hands; it winked back at him, blue and enigmatic, little ribbons of fire crawling in its depth. *Fires to burn his soul to ashes. . . .* Damon clamped his teeth against the cold nausea of his dread. "You'll have to help," he said roughly.

"But how? I know nothing of this."

"Haven't you ever kept watch for Callista when she went *out?*"

Ellemir shook her head. "She never said anything to me of her training or her work. She said it was difficult and she would rather forget it when she was here."

"A pity," Damon said. He settled himself comfortably in his chair. He said, "Very well, I'll have to teach you now. It would be easier if you were experienced in this, but you have enough to do what you must. It is simple. Here. Lay your hands against my wrists, so that I can still see the starstone, but — yes, there, at the pulse spots. Now —" He reached out, tentatively, trying to make a light telepathic contact. She flinched physically, and he smiled. "Yes, that's right, you

71

can perceive the contact. Now all you must do is to keep watch over my body while I am out of it hunting for Callista. When I first go *out,* I will feel cold to your touch, and my heart and pulse will slow slightly. That is normal; don't be afraid. But if we are interrupted, don't let anyone touch me. Above all, don't let anyone move me. If my pulse begins to quicken and race, or if the veins at my temples swell, or my body begins to grow either deathly cold or very warm, then you must wake me."

"How do I do that?"

"Call my name, and put your whole force behind it," Damon said. "You don't have to speak aloud, just project your thoughts at me, calling my name. If you cannot wake me, and it gets worse — for instance, if I show any difficulty in breathing — wake me at *once;* don't delay any further. At the last, but only if you cannot wake me any other way, touch the stone." He winced as he said it. "Only as a last desperate expedient, though; it is painful and might throw me into shock." He felt her hands tremble as they gripped his wrists, and felt her fear and hesitation like a faint fog obscuring the clarity of his own thought.

Poor child. I shouldn't have to do this to her. Damn the luck. If Callista had to get herself into trouble — He forced himself to be fair, and tried to still his pounding heart. This wasn't Callista's fault either. He should save his curses for her kidnappers.

Ellemir said timidly, "Don't be angry, Damon," and he thought, *It's a good sign she can feel that I'm angry.* He said aloud, "I'm not angry at you, *breda.*" He used the intimate word which could mean simply *kinswoman* or, more closely, *darling.* He settled himself as comfortably as he could, sensitizing himself to the feel of Callista's hairclasp between his hands, the starstone above it, pulsing gently in unconscious rhythm with his own nerve currents. He tried to blur everything else, every other sensation, the feel of Ellemir's cold hands on his wrists and her warm breath against his throat, the faint woman-scent of her closeness; he blotted these out, blotted out the flicker of fire and candle beyond them, dimmed the shadows of the room, let vision sink into the blue pulsing of the starstone. He sensed, rather than physically felt, the relaxing of his muscles as his body went insensible. For an instant nothing existed except the vast blue of the starstone, pulsing with the beating of his heart, then his heart stopped, or at least he was no longer conscious of anything except the expanding blueness: a glare, a blue flame, a sea rushing in to drown him. . . .

With a brief, tingling shock, he was out of his body and standing over it, looking down from above, with a certain ironic detachment, on the thin, slumped body in the chair, the frail, frightened-looking girl kneeling and grasping its wrists. He was not really seeing, but perceiving in some strange, dark way through closed eyelids.

In the overlight forming around him he cast a swift downward look. The body in the chair had been wearing a shabby jerkin and leather riding breeches, but as always when he stepped *out* he felt taller, stronger, more muscular, moving with effortless ease as the walls of the great hall thinned and moved away. And this body, if it could be called a body, was wearing a glimmering tunic of gold and green that flickered with a faint firelight glow. Leonie had told him once, "this is how your mind sees itself." He was bare-armed and barefoot, and he felt an incongruous flicker of amusement. *To go out in the blizzard like this?* But of course the blizzard was not *here,* not at all, although if he listened, he could hear the faint howl of the wind, and he knew the violence of the storm must be intense indeed if even its echo could penetrate into the overworld. As he formulated that thought he felt himself begin to shiver and quickly dismissed the thought and memory of the blizzard; his consciousness of it could solidify it on this plane and bring it here.

He moved, gliding, not conscious of separate steps. He was conscious of Callista's jeweled butterfly still between his hands, fluttering like a live thing, beating with the impress of her mental "voice." Or rather, since the jewel itself was in the hands of his body, "down there," the mental counterpart of the ornament which he bore "here." He tried to sensitize himself to the special reverberations of that "voice," adding to it

74

his call, a shout that felt to him like a commanding bellow.

"Callista!"

There was no answer. He had not really expected an answer; if it had been that simple, Ellemir would have already made contact with her twin. Around him the overworld was as still as death, and he looked around, all the time aware that the world, and himself, were only comfortable visualizations for some intangible level of reality. . . . That he saw it as a "world" because it was more convenient to see and feel it that way than as an intangible mental realm; that he visualized himself as a body, striding across a great barren empty plain, because it was easier and less disconcerting than visualizing himself as a bodiless point of thought adrift in other thoughts. At the moment it looked to him like an enormous flat horizon, stretching away dim and bare and silent into endless spaces and skies. In the far distance shadows drifted, and as his curiosity was roused about them, he moved rapidly, without the need to take steps, in their direction.

As he came nearer, they became clearer, human forms which looked oddly gray and unfocused. He knew that if he spoke to them, they would immediately vanish — if they had nothing to do with him or his quest — or immediately come into sharp focus. The overworld was never empty: there were always minds out on the astral for one reason or another, even if they were only sleepers out of their bodies, their

75

minds crossing his in the formless realm of thought. He saw a few faces, dimly, like reflections in water, of people he vaguely recognized. He knew that these were kinsmen and acquaintances of his who were sleeping or deep in meditation, and that he had somehow come into their thoughts; that some of them would wake with a memory of having seen him in a dream. He passed them without any attempt to speak. None of them could have any bearing on his search.

Far in the distance he saw a great shining structure which he recognized from previous visits to this world, and knew it was the Tower where he had been trained, years before. Usually he bypassed it, in such journeys, without passing near; now he felt himself drifting nearer and nearer to it. As he came closer it took on form and solidity. Generations of telepaths had been trained here, exploring the overworld from this base and background. No wonder the Tower stood firm as a landmark in the overworld. Surely Callista would have come here, if she was out on the planes and was free, he thought.

Now he stood on the plain, just below the looming structure of the Tower. Grass, trees, and flowers had begun to formulate around him, his own memory and the joint visualizations of everyone who came into the overworld from the Tower keeping them relatively solid here. He walked amid the familiar trees and scented flowers now with an aching sense of loss, of nostalgia, almost of homesickness. He passed through the dimly shining gateway, and stood briefly on the remembered stones. Suddenly, before him, stood a veiled woman, but even through her veils he knew her: Leonie, the sorceress-Keeper of the Tower during his years there. Her face was a little blurred; half, he knew, the face he remembered; half, the face she wore now.

"Leonie," he said, and the dim figure solidified, took on more definite and clear form, even to the twin copper bracelets, formed like serpents, which she always wore. "Damon," she said, with gentle reproach, "what are you doing out here on this plane tonight?"

He held out the silver butterfly clasp, and felt it cold and solid between his fingers. He said, and heard his own voice strangely thinned, "I am looking for Callista. She is gone, and her twin cannot find her anywhere. Have you seen her here?"

Leonie looked troubled. She said, "No, my dear. We, too, have searched, and she is nowhere on any plane we can reach. From time to time I can feel her somewhere, her living presence, but no matter where I look I cannot come to her."

Damon felt deeply disquieted. Leonie was a powerful, trained telepath, and all the accessible levels of the overworld were known to her. She walked in that world as readily as in the solid world of the body. The fact that Callista's distress was known to her, and that she herself could not locate her pupil and friend, was ominous. Where, in any world, was Callista hiding?

"Perhaps you can find her where I cannot," said Leonie gently. "Blood kin is a deep tie, and may link kindred when friendship or affinity fails. Somehow I think she is there." Leonie raised a shadowy arm and pointed. Damon turned in the direction indicated, and saw only a thick, foggy darkness.

"The darkness is new on this plane," Leonie said, "and none of us can breach it, at least not yet. When we move in that direction we are flung back, as if by force. I do not know what new minds move on this level, but they have not come here by our leave."

"And you think Callista may have strayed into that level and be held there, unable to penetrate that shadow with her mind?"

"I fear so," Leonie said. "If she were kept drugged, or entranced; or if her starstone had been taken from her, or she had been so ill-treated that her mind had been darkened by madness; then it might appear to us, on this level, as if she were imprisoned in a great and impenetrable darkness."

Quickly, with the swiftness of thought, Damon told Leonie what he knew of the abduction of Callista, from her very bed at Armida.

"I do not like it," Leonie said. "What you tell me frightens me. I have heard that there are strange men from another world, at Thendara, and that they have come there by permission of the Hasturs. Now and again one of them strays in a dream on to the overworld, but their forms

78

and their minds are strange and mostly they vanish if one speaks to them. They are only shadows here, but they seem harmless enough, men like any others, without much skill at moving in the realms of the mind. I find it hard to believe that these Terrans — that is what they call themselves — can have had any part in what has happened to Callista. What reason could they have had? And since they are on our world by sufferance, why would they antagonize us by such conduct? No; there seems more purpose to it than that."

Damon became conscious that he was cold again, and shivering. The plain seemed to tremble under his feet. He knew that if he wished to remain in the overworld, he must move on. Speaking to Leonie had been a comfort, but he must not linger here if he hoped to carry on his search for Callista. Leonie seemed to follow his resolution, and said, "Search, then. Take my blessing." Even as she raised her hand in the ritual gesture, her form faded and Damon discovered that he had receded a great distance and was no longer standing on the familiar courtyard stones of the Tower, but had come a long way over the gray plain toward the darkness.

The cold grew and he shuddered with the recurrent blasts, like icy winds, that beat out from that dark place. The darkening lands, he thought grimly, and against the cold he quickly visualized himself dressed in a thick gold and green cloak. The cold lessened, but only slightly, and his motion toward the darkness grew ever slower, as if some pressure from that darkness were flowing out, pushing him backward, backward. He struggled against it, calling out Callista's name again. *If she's anywhere out on the planes, she'll hear that,* he thought. But if Leonie had sought in vain, how could *he* hope to succeed?

The darkness flowed, like thick boiling cloud, and seemed suddenly peopled with dark twisted shapes, menacing half-seen faces, threatening gestures made by bodiless limbs that were seen for a moment in the darkness and vanished again. Damon felt a spasm of fear, an almost anguished longing for the solid world and his solid body and the fireplace at Armida. . . . The world seemed full of half-heard threats and cries. *Go back! Go back or you will die!*

He slogged painfully onward, forcing his way hard against the pressure. Callista's butterfly clasp, between his hands, seemed to shine, and flutter, and vibrate, and he knew that he was coming nearer to her, nearer. . . .

"Callista! Callista!"

For an instant the thick dark cloud thinned, and almost, for a moment, he saw her, a shadow, a wisp, in a thin, torn nightdress, her hair loose and tangled, her face dark and bruised with pain or tears. She stretched out her hands to him, in appeal, and her mouth moved, but he could not hear. Then the darkness boiled up again, and for a moment he saw flashing sword-blades, curiously shaped, slashing.

Quickly, Damon shifted ground again, and with a swift thought, transformed the thick warm cloak into a gleaming coat of armor. None too soon. He heard the half-visible sword-blades clash against it and a nightmarish stab of pain came and went, momentarily, near his heart.

The swords retreated into the darkness, and again he tried to press forward. Then the darkness began to boil up again, like the whirling of a tornado, and out of the thick bubbling whorl of the maelstrom of cloud came a thin, malevolent voice.

"Go back. You cannot come here."

Damon stood his ground, working hard to make the feel of the surface beneath his boots solid, to formulate familiar paving stone so that he and his invisible antagonist stood on ground of his choosing. But beneath him the surface rippled and flowed like water until he felt dizzy, and again the invisible voice spoke, in tones of command.

"Go, I tell you. Go while you still can."

"By what right do you tell me to go?"

The indifferent voice said thinly, "I know nothing of right. I have the power to make you go, and I shall do so. Why provoke such a struggle without need?"

Damon stood his ground, although it seemed as if he were swaying in a sickening up-and-down rhythm, his head pounding with pain. He said, "I will go if my kinswoman comes with me."

"You will go, at once, and that is all I intend to

say," the voice said, and Damon felt an enormous thrust of power, a great blow that sent his head reeling. He struggled inside the boiling darkness, and cried out, "Show yourself! Who are you? By what right do you come here?" The starstone — or its mental counterpart — was still between his fingers; he swung it over his head, like a lantern, and the darkness was illuminated by a dazzling blue glare. By that light he beheld a tall, strangely robed figure, with a savage cat's head, and great claws. . . .

And at that moment there was another of those savage blows. The darkness receded, into a great howling, screaming wind, and Damon found himself alone on what felt like a slippery hillside. Around him was the buffeting wind, the razor-needles of sleet driving into his face . . . the thick driving snow, the storm. . . .

He struggled to regain his footing, knowing that out here he had met something he had never before encountered on this plane. His flesh seemed to crawl, and he tensed himself, knowing that now he must fight for his sanity, his very life. . . .

The telepaths of Darkover were trained to work with the starstones, which had the power, assisted by the human mind, of transforming energies directly from one form to another. In the realms where their minds traveled to encompass this work, there were strange things, intelligences which were not human, or material, but came from other realms of existence. Most of them had nothing to do with humankind at all. Others were prone, when touched by human minds come seeking in the realms to which they, the alien intelligences belonged, to meddle with those human minds. A few of them, reached by human minds trained to reach their levels, remained in contact with the human levels, and were visualized as demons, or even as gods. The Ridenow Gift, Damon's Gift, had been deliberately bred into the minds of his family, to allow them to scent and make contact with these alien presences.

But he'd never seen one who took that form . . . *the great cat.* . . . It was deliberately malevolent, not just indifferent. It had thrust him here, into the level of the blizzard. . . .

He forced himself to search for rationality. The blizzard was not real. It was a thought-blizzard, solidified here by thought, and he could take refuge in other realms where it did not blow. He visualized warm sunshine, a sunlit mountain-side . . . for a moment the snow-needles thinned, then began to rage with renewed force. Someone was projecting it at him . . . someone or *something.* The cat-men? Was Callista in their power, then?

The gusts of wind strengthened, forcing his weakening body to its knees. He struggled, slipped, and fell on rugged ice, which cut him. He felt himself bleeding, freezing, weakening. . . .

Dying. . . .

He thought, with icy rationality, *I've got to get off this level, I've got to get back to my body.* If he was trapped here, out of his body, his body would live a while, spoon-fed and helpless, slowly withering, and finally die.

Ellemir, Ellemir, he sent out the call that sounded like a scream. *Wake me, bring me back, get me out of here!* Again and again he shouted, feeling the howling of the winds carry his cry away into the snow-cut needled darkness. His face was cut, his hands bleeding as he struggled again and again to get to his feet in the snow, to raise himself to his knees, to crawl even. . . .

His struggles grew fainter and fainter, and a sense of total hopelessness, almost of resignation, came over him. *I should never have trusted to Ellemir. She isn't strong enough. I'll never get out.* It seemed he had been sliding, slipping, floundering in the nightmare blizzard for hours, days. . . .

Agony lanced through him, and an icy pain squeezed his head. A glare of blue fire sprang up wildly around him, there was a shock like a thunderclap, and Damon, weak and gasping and exhausted, was lying in the armchair in the great hall at Armida. The fire had long burned down, and the room was icy cold. Ellemir, pale and terrified, her lips blue and chattering, looked down at him. "Damon, oh, Damon! Oh, wake up, wake up!"

He gasped, painfully. He said, "I'm here, I'm back." Somehow, she had reached into the nightmare of the overworld and brought him back. His head and heart were pounding; and his teeth chattering. He looked around. Daylight was beginning to steal through the long windows; outside, the courtyard lay quiet and peaceful in the daybreak; the storm was over, inside and out. He blinked and shook his head. "The blizzard," he said, dimly.

"Did you find Callista?"

He shook his head. "No, but I found whatever has her, and it nearly took me too."

"I couldn't wake you — and you were blue and gasping, and moaning so. Finally I grabbed the starstone," Ellemir confessed. "When I did, I thought you were having a convulsion. I thought I'd killed you —"

She nearly had, Damon thought. But better that than leaving him to die in the raging blizzard of the overworld. She had been crying. "Poor girl, I must have frightened you out of your wits," he said tenderly, and drew her down to him. She lay across his knees, still trembling; he became aware that she was nearly as cold as he was. He caught up a fur lap-robe that lay across the back of the settle, and wrapped it around them both. Soon he would mend the fire; just now it was enough to huddle within its comforting warmth, to feel the girl's icy stiffness begin to lessen a little and her shivering quiet. "My poor little love, I frightened you, and you're half dead with cold and fright," he murmured, holding her tight against him. He kissed her cold, tear-wet cheeks and became aware that he had been wanting to do that for a long, long time; he let his kisses move slowly from her wet face to her cold lips, trying to warm them with his own. "Don't cry, darling. Don't cry."

She stirred a little against him, not in protest but in returning awareness, and said, almost sleepily, "The servants are still abed. We should make up the fire, call them —"

"Damn the servants." He didn't want anyone interrupting this new awareness, this new and beautiful closeness. "I don't want to let you go, Ellemir."

She lifted her lips and kissed him on the mouth. "You don't have to," she said softly, and they lay quietly, close together in the great fur robe, barely touching, but warmed by the contact. Damon was conscious of deathly weariness and of hunger, the terrible depletion of nervous force which was the inevitable penalty of telepathic work. Rationally he knew he should get up, mend the fire, have some food brought, or he might pay in hours or days of lassitude and illness. But he could not bring himself to move, was deeply reluctant to let Ellemir out of his arms. For a moment, letting the exhaustion have its way, he lapsed into brief sleep or unconsciousness.

Ellemir was shaking him, and in the bright hall there was a pounding, a sound, a strange shouting. "Someone is at the door," Ellemir said dazedly. "At this hour? And the servants . . . ? What —"

Damon untangled himself from the robe and stood up, going through the hall to the inner court and through that to the great bolted outer doors. Stiffly, with unpracticed fingers, he struggled with the bolt and drew it back.

On the doorstep stood a man, wrapped in a great fur coat of an unfamiliar pattern, clad in ragged and strange clothing. He said, and his accent was strange and alien, "I am a stranger and lost. I am with the mapping expedition from the Trade City. Can you give me shelter, and send a message to my people?"

Damon looked at him confusedly for a moment. He said at last, slowly, "Yes, come in, come in, stranger; be welcome." He turned to Ellemir and said, "It is only one of the Terrans from Thendara. I have heard of them, they are harmless. It is the wish of Hastur that we show them hospitality when needful, though this one is far astray indeed. Call the housefolk, *breda;* he is probably in need of food and fire."

Ellemir collected herself and said, "Come in; be welcome to Armida and the hospitality of the Alton Domain, stranger. We will help you as we may —" She broke off, for the stranger was staring at her with wide, frightened eyes. He said shakily, "Callista! Callista! You are real!"

She stared at him, as confused as he. She stammered, "No. No, I am not Callista, I am Ellemir. But what can you — what can *you* possibly know of Callista?"

Chapter
FIVE

"I may as well tell you at once that I don't believe a word of it," the girl who called herself Ellemir said.

It's still hard to accept that she isn't Callista. They are so damned *alike!* thought Andrew Carr. He sat back on the heavy wooden bench before the fire, drinking in the growing warmth. It was good to be inside a real house again, even though the storm was over. He could smell food cooking somewhere, and that was wonderful too. It could have been entirely wonderful, except for the girl, who looked so much like Callista and so strangely wasn't; she was standing in front of him, looking down with bleak hostility and repeating, "I don't believe it."

The slender red-haired man, kneeling on the hearth to feed the growing fire (he looked tired, too, and cold, and Carr wondered if he were ill), said without raising his head, "That is unfair, Ellemir. You know what I am. I can tell when I am being lied to, and he's not lying. He *recognized* you. Therefore he must have seen either you, or Callista. And where would one of the

88

Terranan have seen Callista? Unless, as he says, his story is true."

Ellemir's face was stubborn. She said, "How do we know that it is not *his* people who have imprisoned Callista? He comes to us with a wild story that Callista has somehow reached him, guided him when he was lost in the mountains, and saved him from the storm. Are you trying to make me believe that Callista could reach this outworlder, this stranger, when you could not find her in the overworld, and when she could not come through to me, her twin sister? I'm sorry, Damon, I simply cannot believe it."

Carr looked straight at the girl. He said, "If you're going to call me a liar, do it *to* me, not over my head. This story of mine, as you call it, is no pleasure to be telling. Do you think I like to sound like a madman? At first I thought the girl was a ghost, as I told you; or that I was dead already and seeing whatever it is that comes after. But when she saved me from falling with the plane, and then when she guided me to a safe place to wait out the storm, I believed that she was real. I *had* to believe it. I don't blame you for doubting me. I doubted myself, long enough. But it's true. And I suppose you are Callista's kinsfolk; heaven knows you look enough like her for a twin."

Too bad, he found himself thinking, *that this one hasn't a little of Callista's sweet disposition.* Well, at least the man seemed to believe his story.

Damon stood up, leaving the fire to fend for it-

89

self now that it was burning well, and turned to Carr. He said, "I apologize for my cousin's lack of courtesy, stranger. She has endured some difficult days since her sister was taken away, in the night and unseen. It is not easy for her to accept what you say, that Callista could reach your mind when she could not reach her own twin; the bond of the twin-born is believed to be the strongest bond known. I cannot explain it either, but I am old enough to know that there are too many things in this life for any man, or any woman either, to understand them all. Perhaps you can tell us more."

"I don't know what I can tell you," Carr said. "I don't understand it either."

"Perhaps you know something you don't realize you know," Damon said. "But for now, stop badgering him, Ellemir. Whoever and whatever he is, or whatever the many truths of all this may be, he is a guest, and weary and cold, and until he has had his fill of warmth and food, and sleep if he needs it, it is a failure in hospitality to question him. You do the Alton Domain no honor, kinswoman."

Carr followed all this sketchily; there were words that he only partially understood, though in Thendara he had been taught to speak the *lingua franca* of the Trade City, and he could make himself understood well enough. Nevertheless, he realized that Damon was upbraiding the girl who looked like Callista; and she flushed to the roots of her coppery hair. She said

90

(speaking slowly, so that he would be sure to understand), "Stranger, I meant no offense. I am sure that any misunderstandings will become clear in time. For now, accept the hospitality of our house and Domain. Here is fire; food will be brought to you as soon as it is cooked. Have you any other need I have neglected to supply?"

"I'd like to get out of this wet coat," Carr said. It was beginning to steam and drip in the growing warmth of the fire. Damon came to help him unwrap it, and laid it aside. He said, "None of your clothing is fit for the storms of our mountains, and those shoes, now, are fit only for the trashpile. They were never built for traveling in the mountains."

Carr said, with a wry grimace, "I wasn't exactly planning on this trip. As for this coat, it belongs to a dead man, but I was damned glad to have it."

Damon said, "I was not intending to insult your manner of dress, stranger. The fact remains that you are unsuitably clothed, even indoors, and dangerously ill-clad for any return journey. My own clothes would hardly fit you" — Damon looked up with a laugh at the tall Earthman, a head taller than he was and probably half again his weight and girth — "but if you have no objection to wearing the clothes of a servant or one of the stewards, I think I can find something which will keep you warm."

"That's very kind of you," Andrew Carr said. "I've been wearing these since the crash, and a

91

change wouldn't feel bad at all. I could use a wash, too."

"I don't doubt it. Very few, even of those who live in the mountains, survive being caught out in our mountain storms," Damon said.

"I wouldn't have lived through it, if it hadn't been for Callista," he answered.

Damon nodded. "I believe it. The very fact that you, a stranger to our world, survived one of our storms, says much for the truth of what you have told us. Come with me, and I'll find you fresh clothes and a bath."

Andrew followed Damon through the broad corridors and spacious rooms and up a long flight of shallow stairs. He conducted him at last into a suite of rooms with wide windows, covered with heavy woven draperies against the cold. Opening from one of the rooms was a large bathroom with a huge stone tub, sunk deep in the floor. Steam was rising from a fountain in the middle of the room.

"Have a hot bath, and wrap up in a blanket or something," Damon said. "I'll go wake up a few more of the servants, and find some clothes to fit you. Shall I send someone to help you bathe, or can you manage by yourself? Ellemir keeps few servants, but I am sure I can find someone to wait on you."

Andrew assured Damon that he was accustomed to bathing himself without assistance, and the young man withdrew. Andrew took a long, luxurious bath, soaking to the neck in the scalding hot water (*And I thought this place was primitive, good God!*), meanwhile wondering a little about the heating system. The ancient Romans and Cretans on Earth managed to have the most elaborate baths in history, so why shouldn't these people? Downstairs they'd been lighting wood fires, but why not? Fireplaces were considered the height of luxury even in some societies that didn't need them. Maybe they used natural hot springs. Anyhow, the hot water felt good, and he lingered, soaking out the stiffness of days spent sleeping on stone floors, clambering around in the mountains. Finally, feeling incredibly refreshed, he climbed out of the deep tub, dried himself, and wrapped himself in a blanket.

Soon afterward Damon returned. He looked as if he, too, had taken advantage of the time to bathe and put on fresh clothes; he looked younger and less exhausted and spent. He brought an armful of clothing, saying almost in apology, "These are poor enough garments to offer a guest; it is the hall-steward's holiday suit."

"At least they're dry and clean," Andrew said, "so thank him for me, whoever he is."

"Come down to the hall when you're ready," Damon said. "There will be food cooked by then."

Left alone, Andrew got himself into the "hall-steward's holiday suit." It consisted of a shirt and knee-length underdrawers of coarse linen; over which went suedelike breeches, flared somewhat from knee to ankle; a long-sleeved finely embroidered shirt with wide sleeves gathered in at the wrist; and a leather jerkin. There were knitted stockings that tied at the knee, and over them low felt boots lined with fur. In this outfit, which was more comfortable than he had thought when he looked at it, he felt warm for the first time in days. He was hungry, too, and when he opened his door to go downstairs, it was only necessary to follow the good smell of food that was rising. He did wonder, a little tardily, if this would take him, not to the hall, but to the kitchens; but the stairway ended in a corridor from which he could see the door to the Great Hall, where he had been welcomed.

Damon and Ellemir were seated at a small table, and a third chair, empty, was drawn up before it. Damon raised his head in welcome and said, "Forgive us for not waiting for you. But I was awake all night, and very hungry. Come and join us."

Andrew took the third chair. Ellemir looked him over with mild surprise as he sat down, and said, "In those clothes you look quite like one of us. Damon has been telling me a little about your people from Terra. But I had thought that men from another world would be very different from us, more like the nonhumans in the mountains. Are you human in every way?"

Andrew laughed. "Well, I seem human enough to myself," he said. "It would seem more rational for me to ask, are *you* people human too? Most of the worlds of the Empire are inhabited by people who seem to be more or less human, at least as far as the casual observer can tell. Most people believe that all the planets were colonized by a common human stock, a few million years ago. There's been plenty of adaptation to environment, but on planets like Terra, the human organism seems to stay fairly stable. I'm not a biologist, so I can't answer for things like chromosomes and such, but I was told before I came here that the dominant race on Cottman IV was basically human, though there were a couple of sapient peoples that weren't." With a shock, he remembered what Callista had said: that she was in the hands of nonhumans. Surely she would want her kinsfolk to know. But should he spoil their breakfast? Time enough to tell them later.

Damon held a dish toward him, and he served himself with what looked — and later, tasted — like an omelet. It had herbs and unfamiliar vegetables in it, but it was good. There were fruits — the nearest analogy to what he was accustomed to were apples and plums — and a drink he had tasted in the Trade City, with the taste of bitter chocolate.

He noticed, while he ate, that Ellemir was watching him surreptitiously. He wondered if by their standards his table manners were atrociously bad, or whether it was more complicated than that.

Ellemir was still unsettling to him. She was so very like Callista, and yet in some subtle way so unlike. He could look at every feature of her face, and not see a hair's difference from Callista: the broad high forehead, with the hair growing in small delicate tendrils at the hairline, too short to be tucked into the neat braids at the back; the high cheekbones and small straight nose with a dusting of amber freckles; the short upper lip and small determined mouth; and the small, round dimpled chin. Callista had been the first woman he had seen on this planet who had not been abundantly and warmly clad, except for the women working in the central-heated spaceport offices, and those were women of the Empire.

Yes, that was the subtle difference. Callista, every time he had seen her, had been in definite undress, in her flimsy blue nightgown. He had seen almost all of her that there was to see. If any other woman had shown herself to him in that kind of attire — well, all his life Carr had been the kind of man who took his fun where he found it, without getting particularly involved. And yet when he woke and found Callista apparently sleeping at his side, and still half-sleeping had reached for her, he had been distressed and had shared her own embarrassment. Quite simply, he didn't really want her on those terms at all. No, that wasn't quite right. Of course he wanted her. It seemed the most natural thing that he should want her, and she had accepted it that way. But what he wanted was something more. He wanted to know her, to understand her. He wanted her to know and understand him, and care about him. At the very thought that she might have reason to fear some crude or thoughtless approach from him, Andrew had gone hot and cold all over, as if by his own clumsy reactions he might have spoiled something very sweet and precious, very perfect. Even now, when he remembered the brave little joke she had made ("Ah, this is sad! The very first time, the very first, that I lie down with any man, and I am not able to enjoy it!"), he felt a lump in his throat, an immense and completely unfamiliar tenderness.

For this girl, this Ellemir, he felt nothing of that sort at all. If he had waked up and found her asleep in his bed, he would have treated her like any other pretty girl he found there, unless she had some strenuous objection — in which case she probably wouldn't have been there at all. But it would have meant no more than that to him, and when it was over, she would have meant no more to him than any of the various other women he had known and enjoyed for a little while. How could twins have such a subtle difference? Was it simply that intangible known as *personality?* But he hardly knew anything at all of Ellemir's.

So how could Callista rouse in him that enormous and unqualified *yes,* that absolute self-surrender, and Ellemir simply a shrug?

Ellemir put down her spoon. She said uneasily, "Why are you *staring* at me, stranger?"

Andrew dropped his eyes. "Didn't realize I was."

She flushed to the roots of her hair. "Oh, don't

apologize. I was staring too. I suppose, when first I heard of men who had come here from other planets, I halfway expected them to be strange, weird, like the strange creatures of horror stories, things with horns and tails. And here you are, quite like any man from the next valley. But I am only a country girl, and not as accustomed to new things as people who live in the cities. So I am staring like any peasant who never sees anything but his own cows and sheep."

For the first time Andrew sensed a faint, a very faint, likeness to Callista: the gentle directness, the straightforward honesty, without coquetry or wariness. It warmed him to her, somehow, for all the hostility she had shown before.

Damon leaned forward, laying his hand over Ellemir's, and said, "Child, he does not know our customs. He meant no offense. . . . Stranger, among our people it is offensive to stare at young girls. If you were one of us, I would be in honor bound to call challenge on you. Ignorance can be forgiven in a child or a stranger, but I can tell you are not a man who would deliberately offend women; so I instruct you without offense." He smiled, as if anxious to reassure Carr that he really meant none.

Uneasily, Carr looked away from Ellemir. That was a hell of a custom; it would take some getting used to.

"I hope it's polite to ask questions," Andrew said. "I could use some answers. You people live here —"

"It is Ellemir's home," Damon said. "Her father and brothers are at Comyn Council at this season."

"You are her brother? Her husband?"

Damon shook his head. "A kinsman; when Callista was taken, she sent for me. And we, too, would like to ask some questions. You are a Terran from the Trade City; what were you doing in our mountains?"

Andrew told them a little about the Mapping and Exploring expedition. "My name's Andrew Carr."

"Ann'dra," Ellemir repeated slowly, with a light inflection. "Why, that is not so outlandish; there are Anndras and MacAnndras back in the Kilghard Hills, MacAnndras and MacArans —"

And that was another thing, Andrew thought, *the names on this planet. They were a lot like Terran names.* Yet, as far as he had ever heard, this wasn't one of the colonies settled by Terran Empire ships and societies. Well, that wasn't important now.

"Have you had quite enough to eat?" Damon asked. "You are sure? The cold here can deplete your reserves very fast; you must eat well to recuperate."

Ellemir, nibbling at a plate of dried fruit resembling raisins, said, "Damon, you eat as if you had been out in the blizzard for days."

"Believe me, it felt that way," Damon said wryly, and shivered. "I did not tell you everything, because he came and we were distracted, but I was thrust into a place where the storm had gone on, and if you had not brought me back —" He stared at something invisible to Carr or the young woman. "Why don't we move to the fire, and be comfortable," he said, "and then we can talk. Now that you are warm and, I hope, comfortable —" He paused.

Andrew, guessing some formal remark was expected, said, "Very. Thank you."

"Now it is time to go over your story again, from the beginning, and in detail." They moved to the fireside, Andrew on one of the high-backed benches, Ellemir in a low chair. Damon dropped to the rug at her feet, and said, "Now begin, and tell us everything. Especially I want to hear every word you exchanged with Callista; even if you did not understand it, there may be some clue in it which would mean something to us. You said that you saw her first after your plane crashed — ?"

"No, that was not the first time," Andrew said, and told them about the fortune-teller in the Trade City, and the crystal, and how he had seen Callista's face. He hesitated at the thought of trying to tell them exactly how deep that random contact had gone, and finally left it without comment.

Ellemir asked, "And did you accept her as real, then?"

"No," Andrew said. "I thought it was a game — the fortune-telling. Maybe even that the old dame was a procuress, showing me women for

100

the usual reasons. Fortune-telling is usually a swindle."

"How can that be?" Ellemir said. "Anyone who pretended to psi powers which she did not in fact possess would be treated as a criminal! That is a very serious offense!"

Andrew said dryly, "My people don't believe there are any psi powers which are *not* pretended. At that time I thought that the girl was a dream. A wish-fulfillment, if you like."

"Yet she was real enough for you to change your plans and decide to stay here on Darkover," Damon said shrewdly.

Andrew felt uncomfortable under his knowing gaze, and said, "I had nowhere special to go. I'm — what's the old saying? 'I'm the cat who walked by himself and all places are alike to me.' So this place was as good as any other and better than most." (As he said it, he remembered Damon saying, "I know when I'm being lied to," but he couldn't explain it and felt foolish trying.)

"Anyhow, I stayed. Say it seemed like a good idea at the time. Call it a whim."

To Carr's relief, Damon left it at that. He said, "In any case, and for whatever reasons, you stayed. Exactly when was this?" Andrew figured out the time, and Ellemir shook her head in puzzlement.

"At that time, Callista was safe in the Tower. She would hardly have sent any psi message for help and comfort, certainly not to a stranger!"

Carr said stubbornly, "I don't ask you to believe it. I'm trying to tell you just exactly what happened, the way I felt it. *You're* supposed to be the ones who understand psychic things like this." Again, their eyes met in that queer hostility.

Damon said, "In the overworld, time is often out of focus. There may have been some element of precognition, for both of you."

Ellemir flared, "You're acting as if you believe his story, Damon."

"I'm giving him the benefit of the doubt, and I suggest you do likewise. I remind you, Ellemir: neither you nor I can reach Callista. If this man has done so, he may very well be our only link with her. It would be best not to anger him."

She dropped her eyes and said curtly, "Go on. I won't interrupt again."

"So. Andrew, your next contact with Callista was when the plane crashed — ?"

"After the plane crashed. I was lying half conscious on the ledge, and she called to me, and told me to take shelter." Slowly, trying to recall word by word what Callista had said to him, he told of how she had saved him from trying to re-enter the plane a moment before it crashed down into the bottom of the ravine.

"Do you suppose you could find the place again?" Ellemir asked.

"I don't know. The mountains are bewildering, when you're not used to them. I suppose I could try, though the trip was bad enough one way."

"I see no reason why it's necessary," Damon said. "Go on. When did she next appear to you?"

"After the snow began. In fact, just about the time it was working up to blizzard proportions, and I was ready to give up and decide it was all completely hopeless, and the best thing to do was to pick out a comfortable spot to lie down and die."

Damon thought that over a moment. He said, "Then the link between you is two-way. Possibly *her* need established a link with you, the first time. But *your* need and danger brought her to you that time, at least."

"But if Callista is free in the overworld," Ellemir cried out, "why could she not come to you there, Damon? Why could Leonie not reach her? It makes no sense!"

She looked so distressed, so frantic, that Carr could not endure it. It was too much like Callista's weeping. "She told me she did not know where she was — that she was being kept in darkness. If it is any comfort to you, Ellemir, she came to me only because she had tried, and failed, to reach you." He tried to reconstruct her exact words. It wasn't easy, and he was beginning to suspect that Callista had reached his mind directly without too much need for words. "She said something like — I think — it was as if the minds of her kinsfolk and friends had all been erased from the surfaces of this world, and that she had wandered around a long time in the dark looking for you, until she had found herself in communication with me. And then she said that she kept coming back to me because she was frightened and alone" — he heard his own voice thicken and catch — "and because a stranger was better than no one at all. She said she thought she was being kept in a part of that level — overworld you call it? — where her people's minds could not reach."

"But how? Why?" Ellemir demanded.

"I'm sorry," Carr said humbly. "I don't know a thing about it. Your sister had a dreadful time trying to explain even that much to me, and I'm still not sure I've got it straight. If what I say isn't accurate, it's not because I'm lying, it's because I just don't have the language to put it in. I seemed to understand it when Callista was telling me about it, but it's something else to try to tell it in your language."

Ellemir's face softened a little. "I don't think you're lying, Ann'dra," she said, again mispronouncing his name in that strange soft way. "If you'd come here with some evil purpose, I'm sure you could tell much better lies than those. But anything you can tell us about Callista, please try to say it somehow. Has she been hurt, did she seem to be in pain, had she been ill-treated? Did you actually see her, and how did she look? Oh, yes, you must have seen her if you recognized me."

Andrew said, "She did not seem to be injured, although there was a bruise on her cheek. She was wearing a thin blue dress, it looked like a

104

nightgown; no one in her right senses would have worn it out-of-doors. It had —" He closed his eyes, the better to visualize her. "It had some kind of embroidery around the hem, in green and gold, but it was torn and I could not see the design."

Ellemir shivered faintly. "I know the gown. I have one like it. Callista wore it to bed the night we were — raided. Tell me more, quickly!"

"Proof of the truth of his tale," Damon said. "I saw her, only for an instant, in the overworld. She still wore that nightdress. Which tells me two things. He has in fact seen Callista. And — a little more ominous — she cannot, for some reason, although she walks in the overworld as if it were her own courtyard, clothe herself in anything more suitable, even in thought. When I have seen her before this in the overworld, she was clothed as befits a *leronis* — a sorceress," he added to Andrew, in explanation, "in her crimson robes, and veiled as a Keeper should be." He repeated, unwillingly, what Leonie had said: "If she were drugged, or entranced, or her starstone taken from her, or if she had been so ill-treated that her mind had darkened into madness —"

"I can't believe that," Andrew said. "Everything she did was too — too sensible, too *purposeful*, if you will. She guided me to one specific place, in the blizzard; and she came back again, so she could show me where to find food that had been stored there for emergencies. I asked her if she was cold, and she told me it was not cold where she was. Also — when I saw the bruise on her face — I asked, and she told me she had not been hurt or really ill-treated."

Damon said, "Try to remember everything she said to you."

"She told me that the herdsman's hut where I sheltered from the storm was not more than a few miles from here. What she said was, she wished she were there with me in body, so that when the storm was over, in a little while she could be —" he frowned, again trying to remember a communication which now seemed to be more in thoughts than words — "warm and safe and at home."

"I know the place," Damon said. "Coryn and I slept there, when we were boys, on hunting trips. It is something, that Callista could come there in thought." He frowned, trying to add it all up. "What else did Callista say to you?"

It was after that, that I woke and found her sleeping almost in my arms, Andrew thought, *but I'm damned if I'm going to tell you about that. That's strictly between me and Callista.* And yet, if some random thing she had said to him might give Damon a clue to her actual whereabouts — He paused, irresolute.

Damon could clearly see the conflict in his face, and followed it more accurately than Andrew would have believed. He said kindly, trying to spare him, "I can well believe that alone in the dark, and both of you in strange and hostile

106

places, you may well have exchanged —" He paused, and Andrew, sensitized to his mood, knew that Damon was searching for a word which would not trespass too strongly on his emotions. "Exchanged — confidences. You don't have to tell us about that."

Funny, how these people can get so close to you, know almost what you're thinking. Andrew was aware of Damon's attempt not to trespass on his privacy, or on the more intimate things he had shared with Callista. *Intimate . . . funny word when I've never set eyes on her. To have come so close, so close to a woman I've never seen.* He was also aware of Ellemir's sullen face and knew that she, too, sensed something of how close he had come to her twin; and that she did not approve.

Damon, too, sensed Ellemir's resentment. "Child, you should be grateful that anyone, anyone at all, could reach Callista. Just because you could not come to her and comfort her, are you going to resent the fact that a stranger could? Would you rather that she should be all alone in her prison?" He turned back to Andrew and said, as if apologizing for Ellemir, "She is very young, and they are twins. But for your kindness to my kinswoman, I am ready to be your friend. Now, if you can tell me anything she said, about her captors —"

"She said she was in the dark," Andrew said, "and that she did not know precisely where she was, that if she knew precisely, she could have left the place somehow. I didn't quite understand that. She said that since she did not know exactly, her body — that's how she seemed to differentiate it — had to stay where they had confined it. And she cursed them."

"Did she say who they were?" Damon asked.

"What she said made no sense to me," Andrew answered. "She said that they were not men."

"Did she tell you how she knew that? Did she say that she had seen them?" Damon asked eagerly.

"No," Andrew answered. "She said that she had *not* seen them, that she suspected they had kept her in darkness so that she should *not* see them. But she suspected they were not men because —" Again he hesitated a little, trying to find a way to phrase it, and then thought, *Oh hell, if Callista didn't mind talking about it to a stranger it can't be anything to be so embarrassed about.* "She said she knew they were not men because none of them had attempted to rape her. She took it for granted that any man would have done just that, which says something funny about the men of your planet!"

Damon said, "We knew already that whoever would stoop to kidnapping a *leronis,* a Keeper, would be no friend to the people of the Domains. I had surmised that she was stolen, not as any woman might be kidnapped, for revenge, or slavery, but quite specifically because she was a trained telepath. They could not have hoped that she could be forced to use her Keeper's powers against her own people. But if she was kept a prisoner, and her starstone taken from her, she could not be used against them, either. And kidnappers, if they were men, would know that a Keeper is always a virgin; that there was a simpler, less dangerous way to make a Keeper powerless to use her skills against them. A Keeper in the hands of her people's enemies would not long remain a virgin."

Carr shuddered in revulsion. *What a hell of a world, where this kind of war against women is taken for granted!*

Once again Damon followed his thoughts and said, with a little wry twist of his mouth, "Oh, it's neither that easy nor that one-sided, Andrew. The man who tries to ravish a *leronis* has no easy or innocent victim, but takes his very life, not to mention his sanity, in his hands. Callista is an Alton, and if she strikes with her full Gift, she can paralyze, if not kill. It *can* be done, it *has* been done, but it's a more equal battle than you would imagine. No sane man lays hands on a Comyn sorceress except at her own desire. But to anyone who has good reason to fear that a Keeper's powers will be used against him, it may seem worth the danger."

"But," Ellemir said, "she has not been touched, you say."

"She said not."

"Then," Damon said, "I think my first surmise is true. Callista is in the hands of the cat-men, and now we know why. I guessed earlier, when I spoke to Reidel, that somewhere in the darkening lands, someone or something is experimenting with unlicensed and forbidden matrix stones, trying to work with telepath powers; to harness these forces outside the wardenship of the Comyn and the Seven Domains. Men have done this before. But as far as I know, this is the first time any nonhuman race has tried to do so."

Suddenly Damon shuddered, as if with cold or fear. He reached blindly for Ellemir's hand, as if to reassure himself of something solid and warm.

As if, thought Andrew, *he were in darkness and fear like Callista's.*

"And they have done it! They have made the darkening lands uninhabitable to mankind! They can come on us with invisible weapons, and even Leonie could not find Callista when they had hidden her under their darkness! And they are strong, Zandru seize them with scorpions! They are strong. I am Tower-trained, but they flung me out of their level, into a storm I could not overcome. They mastered me as if I were a child! Gods! Gods! Are we helpless against them, then? Is it hopeless?"

He buried his face in his hands, shuddering. Andrew looked at him in surprise and consternation. Then, slowly, he spoke, reaching out to lay his hand on Damon's shoulder.

"Don't do that," he said. "That doesn't help anybody. Look, you just pointed out that Callista still has her powers, whatever they are. And she can reach *me.* Maybe, just maybe — I don't know anything about this kind of thing, or whatever wars and feuds you have in your world, but I do know about Callista, and I — I care a lot about her. Maybe there's some way I can find out where she is — help get her back for you."

Damon raised his face, white and drawn, and looked at the Earthman in wild surmise. "You know," he said to Andrew, "you're right. I hadn't thought of that. *You* can still reach Callista. I don't know why, or how, it happened, or even what we can do with it, but it's the one hope we have. *You can reach Callista.* And she can come to you, when another Keeper can't reach her, when her own twin is barred away from her. It may not be completely hopeless after all."

He reached out and gripped Andrew's hands, and somehow the Terran sensed that for him this was a very unusual thing, that touch, among telepaths, was reserved for close intimacy. It put him almost unendurably in touch with Damon for an instant — Damon's exhaustion and fear, his desperate worry about his young cousins, his own deeper doubts and terrors about his own inability to meet this challenge, his horror of the overworld, his deep and desperate doubts of his very manhood. . . . For a moment Andrew wanted to withdraw, to reject this undesired intimacy which Damon, at the end of his endurance, had thrust on him; then he met Ellemir's eyes, and they were so much like Callista's now, pleading, no longer scornful, so full of fear for Damon (*Why, she loves him,* Andrew thought in a

111

flash; *he doesn't seem much of a man to me either, but she loves him, even if she doesn't know it*) that he could not refuse their plea. They were Callista's people, and he loved Callista, and for better or worse he was entangled in their affairs. *I'd better get used to it now,* he thought, and in a clumsy surge of something almost like affection, he put his arm around Damon's shoulders and hugged the other man roughly. "Don't you worry so much," he said. "I'll do what I can. Sit down, now, before you collapse. What in the hell have you been doing to yourself, anyway?"

He shoved Damon down on the bench before the fire. The unendurable contact lessened, dropped away. Andrew felt confused and a little dismayed at the intensity of the emotion that had surged up. It was like having a kid brother, he thought, cloudily. *He's not strong enough for this kind of thing.* It struck him that Damon was older than he was and far more experienced in these curious contacts, but he still felt older, protective.

Damon said, "I'm sorry. I was out all night in the overworld, searching for Callista. I — I failed."

He sighed, with a sense of utter relief. He said, "But now we know where she is, or at least how to get into contact with her. With your help —"

Andrew warned, "I know nothing about these things."

"Oh, that." Damon shrugged it aside. He looked completely exhausted. He said, "I should

112

have more sense; I'm not used to the overworld anymore. I'll have to rest and try again. Just now, I haven't any more strength. But when I can try again" — he straightened his back — "the damned cat-men had better look to themselves! I know, now, I think, what we can do."

And that, Andrew thought, *is one hell of a lot more than I know. But I guess Damon knows what he's doing, and that's enough for me, for now.*

Chapter
SIX

Damon Ridenow woke and lay for a moment staring at the ceiling. Day was waning; after the strenuous all-night search within the overworld, and the confrontation with Andrew Carr, he had slept most of the day. His weariness was gone, but apprehension was still there, deep within. The Earthman was their one link with Callista, and this seemed so unlikely, so bizarre, that one of these men from another world should be able to make this subtle telepathic contact with one of their own. Terrans, with Comyn *laran* powers! Impossible! No, not impossible: it had *happened*.

He felt no revulsion for Andrew personally, only for the idea that the man was an alien, an off-worlder. As for the man himself, he was inclined rather to like him. He knew that was, at least in part, a consequence of the mental rapport they had, for an instant, shared. In the telepath caste, it was often the accident of possessing *laran*, the specific telepath Gift, which determined how close a relationship would come. Caste, family, social position, all these became irrelevant compared to that one compelling fact; one had, or one did not, that inborn power, and in consequence one was stranger or kinsfolk. By that criterion alone, the most important one on Darkover, Andrew Carr was one of them, and the fact that he was an Earthman was a small random fact without any real importance.

Ellemir, too, had suddenly taken on a new importance in his life.

Being what he was, born telepath and Tower-trained telepath, the touching of minds created closeness, above and beyond anything else. He had felt this for Leonie — twenty years his senior, pledged by law to remain virgin, never beautiful. During his time in the Tower, and for long after, he had loved her deeply, hopelessly, with a passion that had spoiled him for other women. If Leonie had known this — and she could hardly have helped knowing, being what *she* was — it had never made any difference to her. Keepers were trained, by methods incomprehensible to normal men or women, to be unaware of sexuality.

Thinking of that brought him around to thinking again of Callista — and of Ellemir. He had known her most of her life. But he was almost twenty years older than she was. His parents had many times urged him to marry, but the devotion of his first youth had gone up in the white heat of smokeless flame for the unattainable Leonie. Later he had never thought of himself as having much to offer any woman. The intimacy he had known with the others, men and women, in the Tower Circle, minds and hearts open to one another — seven of them come together in a closeness where nothing, however small, could be hidden — and nothing refused or rejected, had spoiled him for any contact lesser than this. Cast out of the Tower, he had known such a desolate loneliness that nothing could dispel it.

Lonely, lonely, all my life alone. And I never dreamed . . . Ellemir, my kinswoman, but a child, only a little girl. . . .

Rising swiftly from his bed, he strode to the window and looked down into the courtyard. *So young Ellemir was not.* She was old enough to care for this vast Domain when her kinsmen were away at Comyn Council. She must be nearly twenty years old. Old enough to have a lover; old enough, if she chose, to marry. She was *Comynara* in her own right, and her own mistress.

But young enough to deserve someone better than I; torn by fear and incompetence. . . .

He wondered if she had ever thought of him as a lover, if perhaps she had known other lovers. He hoped so. If Ellemir cared for him, he hoped it was built on awareness, experience, knowledge of men: not the infatuation of an unawakened girl, which might well dissipate when she knew other men. He wondered. Twin sister to a Keeper, she might somehow have picked up some of Callista's conditioned unawareness of men.

In any case, it was now a full-blown thing between them which had to be faced. The sensitivity, the almost-sexual awareness between them, was something they could no longer ignore, and there was not, of course, any reason to ignore it. It would also heighten their ability to work together in whatever lay ahead; they were committed to find Callista, and the rapport between them would only heighten their contact and strength. Afterward — well, they might never be able to get free of one another. Smiling gently, Damon faced the knowledge that they would probably have to marry; they might never be able to remain apart after this. Well, that would not displease him too much either, unless Ellemir was for some reason unhappy about it.

The awareness of this was still on the surface of his mind when he went downstairs, but the moment he saw Ellemir in the Great Hall it was no longer an apprehension. Even before she raised her serious eyes to his, he knew that all this was something she too had come to realize and accept. She dropped the needlework in her hands and came up to him, snuggling in his arms without a word. He drew a deep breath of absolute relief. After a long time, during which neither of them spoke aloud, standing with linked fingers before the fire, he said, "You don't mind, *breda* — that I'm nearly old enough to be your father?"

"You? Oh, no, no — only if you had been too old to father children, like poor Liriel when they married her off to old Dom Cyril Ardais; *that* would trouble me a little. But you, no, I've never stopped to think whether you were old or young," she said, very simply. "I do not think I would want a lover who could not give me children. That would be too sad."

Damon felt an incongruous ripple of inner laughter. *That* he had never thought about; trust a woman to think of the important things. It was not an unpleasant thought, and it would please his family. He said, "I think we need not worry about that, *preciosa,* when the proper time comes."

"Father will be displeased," Ellemir said slowly, "with Callista in the Tower. I think he had hoped I would stay here and keep his house while he lived. But I have completed my nineteenth year, and by Comyn law I am free to do as I will."

Damon shrugged, thinking of the formidable old man who was the father of the twins. "I have never heard that Dom Esteban disliked me," he said, "and if he cannot bear to lose you, it matters little where we choose to live. Love . . ." He broke off, then with swift apprehension, "Why are you crying?"

She curled closer into his arms. "I had always thought," she said bleakly, "that when I chose, Callista would be the first I would tell."

"You are very close to Callista, beloved?"

"Not as close as some twins," Ellemir said, "since when she went to the Tower, and was pledged, I knew we could never, as so many sisters do, share a lover, or a husband. Yet it seems so sad that this thing that means so much to me, she will not know."

He tightened his clasp on her.

"She shall know," he said. "Be sure of this: she will know. Remember, now we know she is alive, and there is one who can reach her."

"Do you really think this Earthman, this Ann'dra, can help us to find her?"

"I hope so. It won't be easy, but then we never thought it would be easy," he said. "Now, at least, we know it's possible."

"How can it be? He's not one of us. Even if he has some powers or gifts like our *laran,* he doesn't know how to use any of it."

"We'll have to teach him," Damon said. That wouldn't be easy either, he thought. He closed his hand over the starstone on its cord around his neck. It must be done if they were to have the faintest hope of reaching Callista; and he, Damon, would have to be the one to do it. But he dreaded it, Zandru's hells, *how* he dreaded it. But he said calmly, trying to give Ellemir confidence, "Until last night, you yourself never thought you could use *laran;* yet you used it, you saved my life with it."

Her smile wavered, but at least she was smiling again. He said, "So for now let us take what we can have of happiness, and not spoil it with worry, Ellemir. As for the law and the formalities, I expect Dom Esteban will return sometime soon." As he spoke the cold awareness rushed over him again, so that he caught his breath for a moment. *Sooner than I think, and it will not be well for any of us,* he thought but he closed his mind to

119

it, hoping Ellemir had not picked up the thought. He continued: "When your father comes, we can tell him our plans. Meanwhile, we will have to teach Andrew what we can. Where is he?"

"Asleep, I suppose. He, too, was very weary. Shall I send to him?"

"I suppose you must. We have little time to lose," Damon said, "although now we have found each other, I would rather be alone with you a while." But he smiled as he said it. They already shared more than he had ever known with any other woman, and for the rest, there was no urgency. He was no raw youth clutching his girl in haste, and they could wait for the rest. Briefly he picked up a shy thought from Ellemir, *But not too long,* and it warmed him; but he let her go, and said, "There is time enough. Send a steward to bid him come down to us, if he is rested enough. And now, I must think." He moved away from Ellemir and stood looking into the blue-green flames that shot up from the piled resin-treated fuel in the fireplace.

Carr was a telepath, and a potentially powerful one. He had found and held rapport with a stranger, not even blood-kin. A part of the over-world barred even to the Tower-trained might be accessible to him. Yet he was wholly untrained, wholly untaught, and not even inclined to believe very much of these strange powers. With all his heart Damon wished someone else were here to teach this man. The awakening of latent psi

120

powers was not an easy task even for those trained to it, and for an off-worlder, with an unthinkably strange background, without even belief and confidence to help him, it was likely to be a difficult and painful business. Damon had shied away from such contacts ever since he had been dismissed from the Tower Circle. It wouldn't be easy to take them up again, to drop his barriers for this stranger. Yet there was no one else.

He looked around the room, searching. He said, "Have you *kirian* here?" *Kirian,* a powerful drug compounded of the pollen of a rare plant from the mountains, had a tendency, in carefully regulated dosage, to lower the barriers against telepathic rapport. He was not sure whether he meant to give it to Andrew Carr or take it himself, but one way or the other it might make it easier to get through to a stranger. Most deliberate telepathic training was done by the Keepers themselves, but *kirian* could heighten the psi powers, temporarily, enough to make contact possible even with non-telepaths.

Ellemir said doubtfully, "I don't *think* so. Not, at least, since Domenic outgrew the threshold sickness. Callista never needed it, nor I. I will look and see, but I fear not."

Damon felt the cold shudder of fear, gnawing deep in his belly. Blurred a little by the drug, he might have been able to endure the difficult business of directing and disciplining the arousal of *laran* in a stranger. The thought of going through

121

it without some help was almost unendurable. Yet, if it was Callista's only chance —

"You have a starstone," Ellemir said. "You used it to show me what little I could do —"

"Child, you are my blood-kin and we are close enough emotionally — even so, when you gripped the stone, it was agony, more than I can tell you," Damon said gravely. "Tell me. Has Callista any other of the matrix jewels, unused?" If he could get for Carr a blank, unkeyed jewel, perhaps he could work more easily with him.

"I am not sure," Ellemir said. "She has many things I have never seen, nor asked about, because they have to do with her work as Keeper. I wondered why she had brought them here rather than leaving them in the Tower."

"Perhaps because —" Damon hesitated. It was hard to speak of his own days in the Tower Circle; his mind kept shying and skittering away like a frightened horse. Yet somehow he must overcome this fear. "Perhaps because a *leronis*, or even a matrix technician, prefers to keep his, or her, working gear close at hand. I don't quite know how to explain it, but it feels better, somehow, to have it within reach. I do not use my own starstone twice in a year," he added, "yet I keep it here, around my neck, simply because it has been made into a — a part of me. It is uncomfortable, even physically painful, to have it too far from me."

Ellemir whispered, verifying swiftly his guess about her own fast-developing sensitivity: "Oh, poor Callista! And she told Andrew that they had taken her starstone from her —"

Grimly, the man nodded. "So even if she has not been ravished or ill-treated, she is suffering now," he said. *Why should I shrink from a little pain or trouble, to spare her worse?* he thought. "Take me to her room; let me look through her things."

Ellemir obeyed, without question, but when they stood in the center of the room the twin sisters shared, with the two narrow beds at opposite ends of the room, she said in a frightened whisper, "What you said — won't it hurt Callista for you to touch her — the things she uses as a Keeper?"

"It's a possibility," said Damon, "but no worse than she has been hurt already, and it may be our only chance."

My men died because I was too cowardly to accept the thing that I was: a Tower-trained telepath. If I let Callista suffer because I fear to use my skills ... then am I worthless of Ellemir, then am I a lesser thing than any off-worlder ... but, God, I am afraid, afraid. ... Blessed Cassilda, mother of the Seven Domains, be with me now. ...

His even, neutral voice betrayed nothing. "Where does Callista keep her belongings? I can tell yours from hers by their feel, but I would rather not waste time or strength on that."

"The dressing table there, with the silver brushes, is hers. Mine is the other, with the embroidered scarves and the ivory-backed brushes and combs." He could feel the tension and fear in Ellemir's voice, but she was trying to match his cool, dispassionate manner. Damon looked on the dressing table, and rummaged briefly in the drawers. "Nothing here but rubbish," he said. "One or two small matrix jewels, first-level or less, good for fastening buttons, no more. You're sure you never saw where she keeps anything of the kind?" But even before he saw her shake her head, he knew the answer.

"Never. I tried not to — to intrude on that part of her life."

"What a pity I'm not the Terran," Damon said sourly. "I could ask her directly." He clasped his hand, reluctantly, over the starstone which hung on its cord, slowly drew it from the leather pouch, closing his eyes, trying to sense something. As always when he touched the cold, smooth jewel he felt the strange sting of fear. After a moment, hesitantly, he moved toward Callista's bed. It lay still tangled and the bedclothing crumpled, as if no one, servant or mistress, had had the heart to disturb the last imprint of her body there. Damon wet his lips with his tongue, bent and reached under the pillow, then drew back, lifting the pillow gingerly. Beneath it, against the fine linen sheet, lay a small silk envelope, almost — but not quite — flat. He could see the shape of the jewel through the silk.

"Callista's starstone," he said slowly. "So her captors did not take it from her."

Ellemir was trying to remember Andrew's exact words. "He said — Callista did not say her starstone had been taken from her," she repeated slowly. "She said, '*They* could only take my jewels from me lest one of them should be my starstone.' Something like that. So it has been here all along."

"If I had had it, maybe I could have seen her in the overworld," Damon mused aloud, then shook his head. No one but Callista could use her stone. Yet it explained one thing. Without her starstone, she could be concealed in the darkness. If she had been touching it, he could probably have located her; he could have focused his own stone on it. . . . No good thinking about that now. He stretched out his hand to take it, then drew back.

"You take it," he directed, and as she hesitated, "You are her blood-kin, her twin; your vibrations are closer to hers. You can handle it with less pain to her than anyone living. Even through the silk insulation there is some danger, but less from you than anyone else."

Gingerly, Ellemir picked up the silk envelope and slipped it into the bosom of her dress. *For all the good that would do*, Damon thought. Callista, with her starstone, might have been better able to resist her captors. Or maybe not. He was beginning to surmise that it could be she was held prisoner by someone using one of these matrix jewels, someone stronger than herself, who wished mostly to hold her powerless; someone who knew that, free and armed, she would be a danger.

The cat-men. The cat-men, Zandru help them all! But how, and where, did the cat-men get together enough skill and power even to experiment with the matrix jewels? *The truth is,* he thought, *none of us knows a damn thing about the cat-men, but we've made the bad mistake of underestimating them. A fatal mistake? Who knows?*

Well, at least the starstone was not in non-human hands.

They were halfway down the stairs when they heard the commotion in the courtyard, the sounds of riders, the great bell in the court. Ellemir gasped and her hand flew to her heart. Damon felt for an instant that prickle of tense fear; then he relaxed.

"It cannot be another attack," he said. "I think it is friends or kinsfolk, or an alarm would have been rung." *Besides,* he thought grimly, *I felt no warning!*

"I think it is Lord Alton come home," he said, and Ellemir looked startled.

"I sent a message to Father when I sent to you," she said, "but I did not believe he would come during Comyn Council, whatever the need." She ran down the stairs, picking up her gray skirt about her knees; Damon followed more slowly through the great doors into the bricked-in courtyard.

It was a scene of chaos. Armed men, covered in blood, swaying in their saddles. *Too few men,* Damon thought swiftly, *for Dom Esteban's bodyguard, any time.* Between two horses, a litter rudely woven of evergreen boughs had been slung, and on the litter lay the motionless body of a man.

Ellemir had stopped short on the courtyard steps, and as Damon came up, the pallor of her face struck him like a blow. Her hands were clenched into fists at her sides, nails driven into the palms. Damon took her gently by the arm, but she seemed not to know he was there, frozen into herself with shock and horror. Damon went down the steps, looking quickly around the pale, strained faces of the wounded men. *Eduin . . . Conan . . . Caradoc . . . where is Dom Esteban? Only over their dead bodies . . .* Then he caught a glimpse of the swarthy aquiline profile and iron-gray hair of the man in the litter, and it was like a blow to the solar plexus, so painful that he physically swayed with the shock of it. *Dom Esteban! By all the hells — what a time to lose the best swordsman and commander in all the Domains!*

Servants were running about in what looked like confusion; two of the blood-soaked men had slid from their horses, and were cautiously unstrapping the litter. The horses carrying it shied away — *The smell of blood, they never get used to it!* — and there was a sharp cry; the man in the litter began to curse, fluently, in four languages.

Not dead, then, but very much alive. But how badly hurt? Damon thought.

"Father!" Ellemir cried out, and began to run toward the litter. Damon caught and held her before she banged into it. The cursing stopped, like a faucet turned off.

"Callista, child —" The voice was harsh with pain.

127

"Ellemir, Father —" she murmured. They had managed to get the litter down to the ground now, and Damon saw the healer-woman pushing her way through the crowding servants. She said, in her crisp voice, "Move back, this is my business. Domna" — to Ellemir — "this is no place for you, either." Ellemir disregarded the woman, kneeling beside the wounded man. His lips drew back harshly in a grimace meant for a smile.

"Well, *chiya,* I'm here." The bushy eyebrows writhed. "I should have brought more men, though." Damon, looking down over Ellemir's bent back, could see on his face the marks of a long struggle with pain, and something worse. Something like fear. Although, since no one living had ever seen fear on the face of Esteban-Gabriel-Rafael Lanart, Lord Alton, no one knew how fear would have looked on that grim and controlled face. . . .

"Away with you now, child. Battle scenes and blood — no place for a little maiden. Damon, is it you? Kinsman, take the child away from here."

And, besides, you can't curse until she's gone, Damon though wryly, seeing the old man's teeth worrying his lip and knowing Dom Esteban's iron prejudices. He laid his hand an Ellemir's shoulder as the healer-woman knelt down beside Lord Alton, and after a moment she permitted him to draw her away.

Damon looked swiftly around the courtyard. Dom Esteban was not the only wounded, he saw; not even the most gravely wounded. One of the men was helped down from his horse and supported, half carried, by two men, toward the stone seat at the center, where they laid him out full length. His leg was wrapped with a crude bandage, blood soaking through; Damon's stomach turned at the thought of what must lie beneath.

Ellemir, pale but controlled now, was quickly giving orders for hot water, bandage linen, cushions. "The Guardroom is too cold," she said to Dom Cyril, the grizzled old *coridom,* or chief steward. "Carry them into the Great Hall; have beds moved in there from the Guardroom. They can be tended there more easily."

"A good thought, *vai domna,*" said the old man, and hobbled toward the leader of the Guard — now that Esteban was out of it — the *seconde,* or chief officer of the Armida Guardsmen; Eduin the man's name was. He was small and gnarled in stature, broad-shouldered and hawk-faced, a long bloody gash now lending a fierce, wild look to his features. There were rips and slashes in the sleeve of his tunic.

"— invisible!" Damon heard him saying. "Yes, yes, I *know* it's not possible, but I swear, you couldn't see them until they were killed, and then they just — they — well, they fell out of the air. Sir, I swear it's true. You could hear them moving, you could see the marks they left in the snow, you could see them *bleeding* — but they weren't *there!*" The man was shaking all over with reaction, and under the smeared blood his face was dead white. "If it hadn't been for the *vai dom* —" He spoke Dom Esteban's name in his own far-mountain dialect, calling him *Istvan*. "Except for the Lord Istvan, we'd all have been killed."

"No one doubts you," said Damon, stepping forward to grasp the man by the arms; he seemed about to fall. "I met them myself, crossing the darkening lands. How did you escape?" *Not as I did, running away and leaving my men to die.* Suddenly his disgust with himself and his own cowardice rose up and sickened him. He felt for a moment as if he would choke. Before Eduin's words he forced himself to be calm and listen.

"I'm not sure. We were walking our horses, and all at once they all shied, started to bolt. While I was trying to get mine under control, there was this — this *howl,* and Dom Istvan had his sword out and there was blood on it. And this cat-man just — just *materialized* out of the air and fell dead. Then I saw Marcos fall with his throat cut, and heard Dom Istvan yell, '*use your ears,*' and Caradoc and I got back-to-back and started swiping at the air with our swords. There was a sort of a hiss, and I thrust at it, and I felt the blade go in, and there was this cat-thing, dying in the snow, and I — Somehow I got the blade free, and kept cutting at everything I could hear. It was like night fighting —" His eyes fell shut as if for a moment he fell asleep where he stood. "Can I have a drink, Lord Damon?"

Damon broke the eerie paralysis that held him. Servants were running into the court with pails of hot water, blankets, bandages, steaming jugs. He beckoned quickly to one of them, wondering who had had sense enough to order a hot brew of *firi* at this hour. He poured a cupful and thrust it at Eduin. The man swilled down the hot raw spirit as if it were watered wine at a banquet, and stood shuddering. Damon said, "Go into the Hall, man; your wounds can be tended better there." But Eduin shook his head. "Nothing much wrong with me, but Caradoc —" He gestured toward the heavyset brown-bearded man who lay, fists clenched, on the stone bench. "He took a wound in the leg." He strode toward his friend and bent over him.

"The Lord Alton —" Caradoc muttered between clenched teeth. "Is he still alive? I heard him cry out when they picked him up."

"He is alive," Damon said, and Eduin held a cup of the strong liquor to Caradoc's lips. The man gulped at it greedily, and Eduin said, low-voiced, "He'll need it when we move him. Give me a hand, *vai dom*. I'm still strong enough to help carry him, and I'd rather help him myself than leave him to the servants; he took the stroke that was meant for me."

Moving as carefully as he could, Damon helped Eduin support Caradoc's great weight up the stairs and into the Great Hall. Caradoc moaned and muttered, half coherently, as if the raw spirit had loosened his control over himself. Damon heard him mumbling, "Dom Esteban was fighting with his eyes closed . . . killed near a

131

dozen of them . . . a lot of us were dead, and more of them . . . heard them running away, can't blame them, felt like running myself, but one of them got him, he crashed into the snow . . . we were sure he was dead until he started swearing at us. . . ." Caradoc's head fell forward on his chest and he slumped, unconscious, between the two who were carrying him.

With Damon's help, Eduin arranged his comrade carefully on one of the camp-beds which had been hastily set up in the hall, and covered him tenderly with warm blankets. He refused help for himself when Dom Cyril offered bandages and ointments, saying that he was almost unhurt. "— But Caradoc will bleed to death unless someone gets to him at once! Help *him! I did what I could, but it wasn't much in the cold.*"

"I'll do what I can," Damon said, gritting his teeth. He felt sick, but like all Comyn Guardsmen commanding even small detachments, he had had sound training in field-hospital techniques; he had, perhaps, had more than most because his deficiencies in swordplay had made him feel he should have a special skill to counterweight his shortcomings. He saw, out of the corner of his eye, that Andrew Carr had come down into the Great Hall and was staring at the scene of carnage with wonder and horror. He caught a glimmer of thought, *Swords and knives, what sort of a place have I landed in;* then he forgot him completely again. "The healer is with Dom Esteban, but this can't wait. Dom Cyril, give me

132

a hand with these bandages."

For the next hour he had not a breath to spare in thinking of Andrew Carr or even of Callista. Caradoc had a wound in the calf of the leg and another in the upper thigh, from which, despite the rough tourniquet Eduin had tied on, blood still oozed slowly. It was a struggle to stanch the bleeding, and an awkward spot for a pressure bandage: one of the great blood vessels in the groin had been nicked. At last he thought it would hold, and he turned to sewing up the flesh wound in the calf — a messy business and one that always made him feel sick; but by the time he had finished that, blood was oozing again from the wound in the groin. He looked down at the man, bitterly, thinking, *One more for the damned cat-things,* but under Eduin's pleading glance he shook his head.

"No more I can do, *com'ii.* It's a bad place."

"Lord Damon, you're Tower-trained. I have seen the *leronis* stop worse wounds than this with her jewel-stone. Can't you do anything?" Eduin pleaded. He had withstood all attempts to get him to rest, or eat, or leave his friend for a moment.

"Oh, God," Damon muttered. "I haven't the skill or the strength — it's delicate work. I could just as easily stop his heart, kill him —"

"Try, anyway," begged Eduin. "He'll die, anyhow, in a few minutes if you can't stop the bleeding."

No, damn it, Damon wanted to lash out. *Let me*

be, I've done as much as I can. . . .

Caradoc didn't run from the cat-men. He probably saved Esteban's life. Thanks to him Ellemir is not this moment fatherless. Is he still alive? I have had not even an instant to go and see! Reluctantly, he said, "I'll try. But don't hope for too much. It's just a bare chance."

He fumbled with tense fingers for the jewel around his neck, drew it out. *Now I must do the work of a sorceress,* he thought bitterly. *Leonie said it, as a woman I would have made a Keeper. . . .*

He stared into the blue stone, concentrating savagely on controlling the magnetic fields. Slowly, slowly, he focused his heightened psi awareness, carefully down and down, to the molecular level and beyond, feeling the pulsing blood cells, the fumbling heart . . . *careful, careful.* . . . For an instant his mind merged with the unconscious man's, a dim swirl of fear and agony, a growing weakness as the precious life's blood oozed away . . . down and down, into the cells, the molecules . . . the blood vessel severed, broken, the gush, the pressure. . . .

Pressure, now, directly against the severed vessel . . . telekinetic psi force, to hold together, together . . . cells knitting; careful, don't stop the heart; ease up just there. . . . He knew he had not moved a muscle, but it felt as if his hands were *inside* the man's body, gripping tight on the severed vessel. He knew he was holding pure energy against the flowing blood. . . .

With a long sigh, he withdrew. Eduin whispered, "I think the bleeding's stopped."

Damon nodded, exhausted. He said hoarsely, "Don't move him for an hour or so, until the clot's strong enough to hold by itself. Put sandbags around him to keep him from moving accidentally." Once the bleeding was stopped, the wound was no great matter. "Bad place, but it could be worse. Half an inch to one side and he'd have been castrated. Keep him from moving, now, and he'll be all right. In hell's name, man, get up. What are you about —"

Eduin had dropped to his knees. He murmured the ritual formula, "There is a life between us, *vai dom.*"

Damon said sharply, "There may be times coming when we're going to need brave men like the pair of you. Save your life for that! Now, damn it, if you don't go and get yourself some food and rest, I'll knock you down and sit on you. Go on, *teniente* — that's an order!"

Eduin muttered groggily, "Dom Istvan —"

"I'll see what's with him. Go and have your own wound seen to," Damon ordered, and looked around, coming up to sharp focus again. Ellemir, white-faced, was still supervising the placing of beds and coverings for the wounded men, and the bringing of food to the less severely wounded. The healer-woman still sat beside Dom Esteban. Damon went slowly toward her, and noticed, as if his body belonged to someone else, that he swayed as he walked. *I'm not used to this anymore, damn it.*

The healer-woman raised her head at Damon's question. "He's sleeping; he won't answer any questions this day. The wound missed his kidneys, by just a fraction; but I think something's hurt in the nerves of the spine. He can't move his legs at all, not even wriggle a toe. It *could* be shock, but I fear it's something worse. When he wakes — well, either he'll be perfectly all right, or else he'll spend the rest of his life dead from the waist down. Wounds in the spine don't heal."

Damon walked away from the healer-woman in a daze, slowly shaking his head. Not dead, no. But if, indeed, he was paralyzed from the waist, he might as well be, would probably rather be. He didn't envy whoever it was that would have the task of telling the formidable old man that his daughter's rescue must be left in other hands.

Whose hands? Mine? Damon realized, with shock, that ever since he had realized that Esteban lived, he had hoped that his older kinsman — who, after all, was Callista's father, her nearest kinsman, and thus in honor bound to avenge any hurt or dishonor to her — would be able to take over this frightful task. But it hadn't happened like that.

It was still up to him — and to the Earthman, Andrew Carr.

He turned resolutely and left the Great Hall to go in search of Andrew Carr.

Chapter
SEVEN

What kind of a world is this, anyway? Swords and knives — bandits, battles, kidnappings. Carr had seen the wounded men, but had quickly discovered that he was only in the way, that his hosts had no time or thought for him now, and had retreated upstairs to the room where they had taken him. He had felt strange about not offering to help, but the place was crawling with people and they all knew more about what to do than he did. He decided the best thing he could do was to keep out of the way.

What was going to happen now? He had gathered, from what little he could understand of the servants' talk — mostly in a dialect he could barely follow — that this was the Lord of this estate: Ellemir's father. With the owner returned, would Damon still be in charge of whatever arrangements could be made for Callista's rescue? It was Callista he was thinking about, almost to the exclusion of everything else. Then, almost as if his thoughts had drawn her to him (maybe they had, she seemed to think there was some such bond between them), he saw her standing before his bed.

137

"So you are safe, safe and well now, Andrew. Have my kinsfolk been hospitable to you?"

"They couldn't have been kinder," Andrew said. "But if you can come into their house, why can't *they* see you?"

"I wish I knew. I cannot see them, I cannot feel their thoughts; it is as if the house were empty, without even a ghost to haunt it! Or as if I were the ghost haunting it — my own house!" Her face crumpled with sobbing. "Somehow, someone has been able to barricade me from everyone, everyone I know. I wander in the overworld and I see only strange, drifting faces, never even a glance from any familiar face. I wonder if I have gone mad . . . ?"

Andrew said slowly, trying to explain the things Damon had told him, "Damon believes you are in the hands of the cat-men; it seems that they have attacked others, and that they keep you prisoner so that you cannot use your starstone against them."

Callista said slowly, "Before I left the Tower, Leonie said something of this. She said that something was amiss in the darkening lands and she suspected that some unmonitored stones were being used — or misused — there. You are a Terran — do you know what I mean by the stones?"

"Not a word of it," Andrew confessed.

"It is the ancient knowledge — science, you would say — of this world. The matrix stones, starstones we call them among ourselves, can be attuned to the human mind, and amplify what you call psi powers. They can be used to change the form of energy. All matter, all energy and force, is nothing but vibration, and if you change the rate at which it vibrates, then it takes another form."

Andrew nodded. He could follow that. It sounded as if she were trying, without the scientific training of the Terran Empire, to explain the atomic field theory of matter and energy; and doing it better than he could do it with the scientific training he had had. "And you can use these stones?"

"Yes. I am a Keeper, and Tower-trained; the leader of a circle of trained telepaths who use these stones for the transmutation of energy. And all the stones we use, keyed to our own individual brains, are monitored from one or another of the Towers; no one is allowed to use them unless he has been personally trained by an older Keeper or technician, and we are sure he will damage nothing. The stones are very, very powerful, Andrew. The higher-level ones, the larger ones, could shatter this planet like a roasting bird bursting in the oven. This is why we were frightened when we discovered that someone, or some*thing*, in the darkening lands was probably using a very powerful stone, or stones, unmonitored and without training."

Andrew was trying to recall Damon's words. "He said men have done this before, but nonhumans never."

"Damon has forgotten his history," Callista said. "It is well-known that our ancient forebears first received the stones from the *chieri* folk, who knew how to use them when we were savages, and have gone so far beyond them that they no longer need them. But the *chieri* have little to do with mankind these days, and few men living have so much as seen one. I wish I might say the same of the cat-things, curse them!" She drew a long, exhausted breath. "Oh, I am weary, weary, Andrew. Would to Evanda I might *touch* you. I think I shall go mad, alone in the darkness. No, I have not been ill-treated, but I am so tired, so tired of the cold stone, and the dripping water, and my eyes ache with the darkness, and I cannot eat the food or drink the water they give me, it is foul with their stink —"

It drove Andrew half mad to hear her sobbing, and to be unable to reach her, touch her, comfort her somehow. He wanted to take her in his arms, hold her close, quiet her crying. And she stood there before him, looking so real, so solid, he could see her breathing and the tears that kept rolling down her face, and yet he could not so much as touch her fingertips. He said helplessly, "Don't cry, Callista. Somehow Damon and I will find you, and if he won't, I'll damn well try it myself!"

Raising his eyes suddenly, he saw Damon standing in the doorway. Damon's eyes were wide. He said, on an indrawn breath of amazement, "Is Callista *here?*"

140

"I can't believe you can't see her," Andrew said, and felt again that strange, tentative outreach of contact, like a touch directly on his mind — he didn't resent it. At least Damon could know that he was telling the truth.

"I never really doubted you," Damon said, and his eyes were wide with wonder and dismay.

"Damon is here? Damon!" Callista said, and her lips trembled. "You say he is here and I cannot see him. Like a ghost, a ghost in my own house and my brother's room —" She made a desperate attempt to control her weeping. Andrew felt the desperation of her struggle to stay calm. "Tell Damon he must find my starstone. *They* did not find it; I was not wearing it. Tell him I do not wear it around my neck as he does his own."

Andrew repeated this aloud to Damon. He felt uncomfortably like a trance medium supposedly relaying messages from a disembodied spirit. The thought made him shudder; they were usually dead.

Damon touched the thong around his neck and said, "I had forgotten she knew that. Tell her Ellemir has it, she found it beneath her pillow, and ask —"

Andrew repeated his words, and Callista interrupted him. "That explains why — I knew *someone* had touched it, but if it was Ellemir —" Her shadowy form wavered and flickered, as if the effort to stay present with them had taxed her beyond endurance. To Andrew's quick cry of

141

concern she whispered, "I am very weak — I feel as if I were dying — or perhaps . . . Watch the stone," and she was gone. Andrew stood looking, in terror, at the place where she had disappeared. When he repeated her words Damon ran down the corridor, shouting for Ellemir.

"Where were you?" he demanded irascibly, when finally she appeared.

She looked at him in astonishment and annoyance. "What is the matter with you? My clothes were soaked in blood; I have been tending wounded men. Have I no right to a bath and clean garments? I sent the very servants for so much!"

How like and how unlike Callista, Andrew thought, and felt a completely irrational resentment, that this one was walking around free, enjoying a bath and fresh clothes and Callista was alone and crying in the dark somewhere.

"The starstone, quickly," Damon demanded. "We can see in it if Callista is alive and well." He explained to Andrew, quickly, that when a trained matrix worker died, his starstone "died" too, losing color and brilliance. Ellemir drew it out, handling it gingerly through the insulating silk, but it pulsed as brightly as ever.

Damon said, "She is exhausted and frightened, it may be, but she is physically very strong, or the stone could not shine so brightly. Andrew! When she comes to you again, tell her that she must somehow force herself to eat and drink, to be strong, to keep her strength up until we can somehow come to her! I wonder why she was so insistent that we must find her starstone?"

Andrew stretched out his hand to it, and said, "May I — ?"

"It is hardly safe," Damon said hesitantly. "No one can use a stone keyed to another." Then he remembered. Callista was a Keeper, and they were so highly trained that, sometimes, they could key themselves in to someone else's stone. Leonie had held his in her hands many times, and while Ellemir's lightest touch on it, even though it had saved his life, had been agony, Leonie's had hurt him no more than the touch of Leonie's hand on his cheek. During his training, before they taught him how to key his own starstone to the rhythm of his own brain and energies, he had been trained with his Keeper's stone; and for that time he had been so in touch with Leonie that they were wide open to one another. *Even now a thought will bring her to me,* he thought.

Andrew knew what Damon was thinking. *It's as if he were broadcasting his thoughts to me. I wonder if he knows it?* He said quietly, "If Callista and I weren't awfully close in touch somehow, I don't think she'd keep coming back to me." He hesitated a moment, reluctant to reveal more, then realized that for Callista's sake, for all their sakes, it was unfair to keep back even what should have been private and highly personal. He said, trying to keep his voice even, "I — I love her, you know. I'll do whatever you think is best

143

for her, no matter what it takes. You know more about this kind of thing than I do. I'm completely in your hands."

For an instant Damon felt a sting of revulsion (*This alien, this stranger, even his thoughts defile a Keeper*), then he made himself be fair. Andrew was not a stranger. However it had happened, however it came about, this alien, this Earthman, had *laran*. As for loving a Keeper, he himself had loved Leonie all his life, and she had never been angry about it or felt it an intrusion, even though she had never responded even a breath to his desire; his love she had accepted, although in an entirely sexless way. Callista was probably equally capable of defending herself, if she wished, against this stranger's emotions.

Andrew was getting very tired of seeing everything that happened through Damon's eyes. "One thing I *don't* understand," he said. "Why must a Keeper necessarily be a virgin? Is it a law? Something religious?"

"It has always been so," said Ellemir, "from the most remote past."

That, of course, Andrew thought, wasn't a reason.

Damon sensed his dissatisfaction and said, "I don't know if I can explain it properly — it's a matter of nerve energies. People have only so much. You learn to protect your energy currents, how to use them most effectively, how to relax, to safeguard your strength. Well, what uses most human energy? Sex, of course. You can *use* it,

144

sometimes, to channel energy, but there are limits to that sort of thing. And when you're keyed into the matrix jewels — well, the energy *they* will carry is limitless, but human flesh and blood and brainwaves can stand only so much. For a man it's fairly simple. You can't overload with sex because if you're too heavily over-loaded, you simply can't function sexually at all. Matrix telepaths find that out fairly early in the game. You have to go on short rations of sex if you want to keep enough energy to do your work. For a woman, though, it's easy to — well, to overload. So most of the women have to make up their minds to stay chaste, or else be very, very careful not to key into the more complex matrix patterns. Because it can kill them, very quickly, and it's not a nice death."

He remembered a story Leonie had told him, early in the training. "I told you, once, that it wasn't easy to ravish a Keeper, unwilling — but that it could be done, it *had* been done. There was a Keeper once — she was a princess of the House of Hastur — and it was during one of the wars, when such women could be used as pawns. So the Lady Mirella Hastur was kidnapped, and they flung her out at the city gates, believing she was now useless to work against them. But the other Keeper in the Tower had been killed out-right, and there was no one to act against the in-vaders who were storming Arilinn. So the Lady Mirella concealed what had been done to her, and went into the screens, and fought for hours

145

against the forces mustered against them. But when the battle was over and the invaders lay, all of them, dying or dead at the city gates, she came down from the screens, and fell dead at their feet, burned out like a spent torch. Leonie's grandmother was a *rikhi,* and Under-Keeper, at that time, and she saw the Lady Mirella die, and she said that not only was her starstone blasted and blackened, but that the Lady's hands were burned as with fire and her body scorched by the energies she could no longer control. There is a monument to her in Arilinn," he concluded. "We pay our respects to her memory each year at Festival Night, but I still believe it is there as a warning to any Keeper who trifles with her powers — or her chastity."

Andrew shuddered, thinking, *Maybe it's just as well I couldn't touch Callista even for a moment. I wonder, though, if Damon told this story to keep me from getting ideas later on!*

Damon gestured to Ellemir and said, "Give him the stone, child. Touch it lightly at first, Andrew. Very lightly. Your first lesson," he added wryly. "Never grasp a starstone hard in your hands. Handle it, always, as if it were a living thing." *Must I, too, work as a Keeper? To train him, as Leonie trained me?*

Andrew took the stone from Ellemir's outstretched fingers. He had caught Damon's resentful thought and wondered what the slender Comyn Lord was angry about. Were all the telepaths women here, so Damon felt that being one made him less of a man? No, it couldn't be that, or he wouldn't have one of the stones himself, but Andrew felt there was *something*. The starstone felt faintly warm, even through the silk. He had somehow expected it to feel like any other jewel, cold and hard. Instead it had the warmth of a live thing in his palm.

Damon said, in a low voice, "Now take off the silk. Very gently and slowly. Don't look at the stone right away."

He unwrapped the insulating silk, and saw Ellemir flinch. She said in a low voice, "I felt that."

Damon said swiftly, "Cover it again, Andrew." He obeyed, and Damon asked, "Did it hurt when he touched it?"

Can we use Ellemir as a barometer to Callista's reactions? Andrew thought.

"It didn't exactly *hurt*," Ellemir said, her brow knitted, evidently trying to be very exact about her reactions. "Only — I *felt* it. Like a hand touching me. I'm not sure where. It wasn't even really unpleasant. Just — somehow, intimate."

Damon frowned slightly. "You're developing *laran*," he said. "That's evident. That may be helpful."

She looked frightened and said, "Damon! Is it — dangerous for me? I am no virgin."

Twin to a Keeper and so ignorant? Damon thought in exasperation, then saw that she was really afraid. He said quickly, "No, no, *breda*. Only for those women who work at the highest levels in the screens or with the most powerful stones. You might, if you overworked — and you were exhausted with lovemaking, or pregnant — get a bad headache or a fainting fit. Nothing worse. There are women, Tower-trained, working among us there, who need not live by a Keeper's laws."

She looked relieved and faintly embarrassed. It was evidently not, Andrew thought, the kind of thing girls here usually blurted out in front of strangers. Although sexual taboos here seemed to be different than they were among Terrans, they seemed to have plenty of them.

Damon said, "Ellemir, touch my stone a moment. Lightly — careful," he said, gritting his teeth as he unwrapped the stone.

Andrew, watching, thought he was braced as if for a low blow. Ellemir laid her fingertip lightly on the stone, and Damon only sighed a little.

So Ellemir and I are keyed together somehow, he thought. *It's understandable. It always happens in sympathy like this. If we came closer still, if I took her to my bed, perhaps she could even learn to use it. Well, if I needed a good reason . . .* He laughed a little, harshly, aware that once again he was broadcasting his thoughts both to the woman who was their subject and to the man who was still, by ordinary standards, a stranger. Well, they'd all better get used to it. It would be worse before it was better.

"For what it's worth," he said aloud, and Andrew heard the tension and fear in his voice, "it

148

seems Ellemir can handle my stone without hurting me. Which helps. As for you, Andrew, I *think* I can key you into Callista's stone without danger to her. It's a risk we'll have to take. You're our one link with her. For what we're going to have to do —"

Andrew looked quizzically at the older man and asked, "Precisely what *are* we going to do?"

"I'm not sure yet. I can't make definite plans until Dom Esteban wakes. Her father has a right to share in any plans we make." *Besides,* Damon thought grimly, *by then we'll know whether or not he can take any part in the rescue.* "But whatever we do, Callista will have to know about it. And, anyway" — he saw Ellemir flinch as he said it — "even if Callista should be hurt, or killed, we would still have to go out against whomever is doing this in the darkening lands."

Andrew thought, *I'm only in this for Callista's sake; I want no other part of it.* But before Damon's haggard face he could not bring himself to say so. He was still holding the wrapped stone.

Damon sighed deeply and said, "Unwrap it again. Touch it — lightly. Ellemir?" He glanced at the woman, and she nodded.

"Yes. I feel it when he touches it, still."

Andrew gingerly held the stone between his palms. He was seated on a low chair near the window, Damon standing before him. Damon said grimly, "I'd better guard against what happened last time." He dropped cross-legged on the thick carpet, drawing Ellemir down beside him.

Andrew, watching Damon's face, thought, *He's afraid. Is it that dangerous?*

Damon's gray eyes met the Earthman's, as he said, "Don't deceive yourself; yes, it is. People who use these skills without adequate training can do immense harm. I ought to tell you there's some risk to you, too. Usually the business of keying anyone into a matrix is handled by a Keeper. I'm not." *Leonie said, if I had been born a woman, I'd have made a Keeper.* For the first time this thought did not bring Damon the usual ration of self-contempt, doubt of his own manhood. Instead, he felt faintly grateful. It could save all their lives.

Andrew leaned over him, Callista's stone still cradled in his hands, and said, "Damon. You know what you're doing, don't you? If I didn't trust you, I'd never have let you start this. Let's take the risk for granted and go on from there."

Damon sighed and said, "I guess that's the only thing we can do. I wish —" but he did not finish the sentence.

I wish there was time to send for Leonie, bring her here. But would she approve of what I am doing — keying in a stranger, a Terran, into a Keeper? Even to save Callista's life? Callista knew what risks a Keeper must take, before ever she pledged to the Tower. Leonie does not know this Earthman as I do, as Callista does.

I have never done anything against Leonie's will,

150

in all my life. Yet she set me free to use my own judgment, and that is exactly what I must do now.

Andrew said, in a low voice, "Exactly what do I have to do? Don't forget I don't know a damned thing about these psychic things." His fingers moved unsteadily on the starstone; remembering Damon's caution, he carefully relaxed his fingers. He thought, *It's as if — I must be as cautious as if it were Callista's own life I were holding between my hands.* The thought filled him with an inexpressible tenderness, and Ellemir raised her head and her gray eyes met his in a brief moment of sympathy. *She is more like Callista than I thought.*

Damon said, "I'm going to go into your mind — make my brain waves, the electrical forcefield of my brain, resonate in the same wavelength of yours, if it's easier to understand it that way — and then try to adjust the field of *your* brain to that of Callista's stone, so that you'll be able to function on that exact frequency. This will put you in closer contact with her, so that, perhaps, you can lead us to her."

"You don't know where she is?"

"I know only in a general way," Damon said. "You told me she spoke of dripping water and darkness. That sounds to me like the caves of Corresanti; they are the only caves within a day's ride, and they would not dare to keep her aboveground and in the light of the sun. And the village of Corresanti is within the borders of the darkening land. But if you are keyed into her

151

starstone, you will be able to use it as a beacon, and find out *exactly* where they have hidden her. And then you can tell us."

Andrew followed all this with some difficulty. He said, "You are evidently an expert with these stones. Why can't you find her with it?"

"Two reasons," Damon said. "Whoever's holding her prisoner is not only holding her body prisoner, and in darkness, but they've managed to barrier her mind on a level of the overworld none of us can reach. Don't ask me how they did it. Whoever's doing this is evidently using a very powerful matrix himself." *The Great Cat I saw,* he thought. *Well, maybe we'll singe his whiskers for him.*

"Second reason. She's evidently in very close touch with you, emotionally. So that half our work is done already. If we had a blank stone for you, I could simply key *your* frequencies into it, and you could lead us to Callista because you are already in touch with her. But since we must use Callista's own stone, which is keyed into *her,* body and brain, we must take into account that only someone in deep sympathy with her can use it without danger. Without you, I might have tried it with her twin. But the fact that Callista can come directly to you means you are the logical one." Abruptly Damon said, "I'm putting it off again. Look into the stone."

Andrew lowered his eyes to the flashing luminescence of blue. Deep inside the stone small ribbons and worms of color moved, slowly, like a beating heart. Callista's heart.

"Ellemir. You'll have to monitor us both." Damon longed, with an almost physical longing, for the trained women from the Tower Circles, who knew this work and could keep in touch, almost automatically, with up to seven or eight telepaths working in the Circle at once. Ellemir was new to *laran*, just awakened, and untrained. "If either of us forgets to breathe, if we seem to be in any deep physical distress, you'll simply have to bring us out of it."

She looked scared, too. "I'll — try."

"You'd better do more than try. You have the talent. *Use* it, Ellemir, as you value your sister's life. Or mine. If you had training, you could step in and regulate our breathing and our heartbeats if they began to go astray; but I'll manage if you can just bring us up to surface if that happens."

"Don't scare her," Andrew said gently. "I know she'll do the best she can."

Damon drew a deep breath, focused deeply on the stone. Fear surged up like a struck flame on flint, and he felt his heartbeat catch, then he forced it back. *I can do this. I used to. Leonie said I could.* He felt his breathing quiet as he relaxed, felt his heartbeats quiet into the slow pulsing rhythm of the stone. He began to try to formulate his instructions to Andrew. *Watch the lights in the stone. Try to quiet your mind, to feel your whole body pulsing in that rhythm.*

Andrew felt the thought — *pick up the beat* — and wondered exactly how it was done. Could you change your own heartbeat that way? Well, in the Medic and Psych Center he'd been taught on a biofeedback machine to initiate alpha rhythms for sleep or deep relaxation. This wasn't all that different. He watched, trying to relax, as he tried to feel and sense the exact rhythmic pulse of the stone. *It's like feeling Callista's heartbeat.* He became conscious of his own heartbeat, of the rhythm of the blood in his temples, of all the small interior noises and feelings and rhythms. The pulse of the starstone between his palms quickened and brightened, quickened and brightened, and he was conscious of his own internal rhythms in a definite, out-of-phase counterpoint. *I guess what I have to do is match those rhythms.* He began breathing deep and slow, trying to match his breathing, at least, to the rhythm of the starstone. *Callista's rhythm? Don't think. Concentrate.* He managed to match his breathing to the exact rhythm of the stone. For an instant it faltered, went ragged, and he felt the spurt of adrenalin through him — *Callista?* — and realized that Ellemir had drawn a deep breath, audible, almost a gasp. He steeled himself to quiet again, tried to pick up the ragged rhythm, slowly returned it to normal. To his own detached wonder, he saw that as his breathing quieted the pulse in the starstone quieted, too.

Now breathing and the pulse of the stone were one rhythm, but his heartbeat was a strong counter-rhythm against the matched beat of stone and breath. *Concentrate. Pick up the beat.*

His eyes were aching, and a wave of nausea rippled through him. The stone was spinning — he squeezed his eyes shut, fighting the surging sickness, but the light and the crawling colors persisted through his closed eyelids.

He moaned aloud, and the sound broke the growing beat to fragments. Damon quickly raised his head, and Ellemir looked up in apprehension.

"What's wrong?" Damon asked softly, and Andrew muttered with difficulty, "Seasick." The room seemed to be swinging in slow circles around him and he held out one hand to brace himself. Ellemir looked pale, too.

Damon wet his lips and said, "That happens. Damn. You're too new to this. I wish — Aldones! I wish we had some *kirian*. Failing that — Ellemir, are you sure there is none here?"

"I honestly don't think so."

Damon thought, *I'm not feeling so good myself. It's not going to be easy.*

Andrew asked him, "Why should it have that effect?" Then he felt Damon's surge of impatience: *Is this the time for asking foolish questions?* His anger, Andrew thought in slow incredulity, looked like a pale red glow around him. "The room's — ragged," he said, and leaned back, closing his eyes.

Damon forced himself to be calm. This was not going to be easy even if they were all in total harmony. If they started arguing, it wasn't even going to be *possible*. And he couldn't expect Andrew, doing a difficult and unexpected thing with total strangers, and struggling against the sickness and pain of having the unused psi centers of his brain forced open, to stay in control. The job of staying in control was strictly up to him. That was a Keeper's job, holding everyone in rapport. *A woman's job. Well, man or woman, right now it's my job.*

He forced himself to relax, deliberately quieted his breathing. He said, "I'm sorry, Andrew. Everybody goes through it sometime or other. I'm sorry it's so rough on you; I wish I could help. You're feeling sick because, first, you're using part of your brain that you usually *don't* use. And, second, because your eyes, and your balance centers, and all the rest of it, are reacting to your effort to bring some — well, some automatic functions under deliberate, voluntary control. I don't mean to be irritable. There's a certain degree of physical irritability I can't quite control either. Try not to focus your eyes on anything, if you can help it, and lie back against the cushions. The sickness will probably go away in a few minutes. Do the best you can."

Andrew stayed still, eyes closed, until the swaying sickness receded a little. *He's trying to help.* The physical sensations were like bad side effects of some drug, a nausea that wasn't even definite enough to be relieved by vomiting, a strange sensation of crawling in his very bowels, strange flashes of light against the inside of his eyes. Well, it wouldn't kill him; he'd had bad hangovers that were worse. "I'm all right," he said, and caught Damon's surprised, grateful glance.

"Actually it's a good sign you should be sick at this stage," he said. "It means something's actually *happening*. Ready to try again?"

Andrew nodded and, without instructions this time, tried to focus on the beat and rhythm within the matrix stone. It was easier now. He realized he did not have to look into the stone; he could sense the pulsation through the tips of his fingers. No, the sensation was not exactly physical; he tried to identify exactly where it came from and lost it again. Did it *matter* where it came from? The important thing was to stay open to it. He picked it up again (*A part of my brain I've never used before?*) and felt how quickly the breathing went into synchronization with the invisible pulsation. After a short, slow time, during which he felt as if he were groping in the dark for an elusive rhythm, the heartbeat followed.

He fought in the dark for what seemed a long time against the elusive cross-rhythms which seemed now to be inside him, now outside. No sooner would he tame one rhythm of the multiplex percussion orchestra and subdue it into the pervasive harmony, than another would escape him and start up a rebellious tickety-tock pattern against it; then he had to listen and analyze them and, somehow, delicately, try to fasten on where in his body the alien rhythm was beating, and try to tune it, beat by rebellious beat, into the proper harmony. After a long, long time he was conscious of beating all in one pulsation, other rhythms quieted, swaying up and down as if cradled inside the vast ticking heart, swaying in a ceaseless, tideless sea, his body and brain, his flowing pulsing blood, the incessant motion of the cells inside his muscles, the slow gentle pulse inside his sexual organs, all pulsing in rhythm. . . . *As if I were inside the jewel, flowing with all the little lights.* . . .

Andrew — the most delicate of whispers, part of the great rhythm.

Callista? Not a question. No answer needed. *As if we lay cradled together in a vast swaying darkness. Yes, that will come too. Cradled like twins in one womb.* He had no conscious thoughts at that moment, lying deep below the level of thought where there was only a sort of unfocused *awareness.* With a small detached level of fragmentary thought, he wondered if this was what was meant by being attuned to someone else's mind. Not conscious of the answer as a separateness, he knew, yes, he was close in contact with Callista's mind. For an instant he sensed Ellemir, too, and without really willing it, a thought tangled through his mind, a flash of faintly disturbing intimacy, as if in this pulsating darkness he lay naked, stripped as he had never been, entangled in intimacy that was like a pounding rhythm of sex. He was aware of both women, and it seemed completely natural, a part of reality without surprise or embarrassment. Then he slipped one notch farther up into awareness and knew his body was there again, cold and soaked in sweat. At that moment he was aware of Damon close by, a disturbing intimacy, not wholly welcome because it thrust between his intense emotional closeness to Callista. He didn't want to be that close to Damon: it wasn't the same, his texture was different somehow, disturbing. For an instant he struggled and felt himself gasp, almost retching, and it was as if the heart between his hand struggled and beat hard for an instant, and then, abruptly, there was a short bright flare of light and a fusion. (For an instant he saw Damon's face and it felt terrifyingly like looking into a mirror, a swift touch and grip and flare.) Then, abruptly and without transition, he was fully conscious of his body again and Callista was disappearing.

Andrew lay back in his chair, aware that he still felt sick. But the acute sickness was gone. Damon was kneeling upright beside him, looking down into his eyes with anxious concern.

"Andrew, are you all right?"

"I'm — fine," he managed to say, feeling a tardy embarrassment. "What the hell —"

Ellemir — he realized suddenly that her hand lay in his, and the other hand in Damon's — gave his fingers a soft little squeeze. She said, "I couldn't see Callista. But she was *there* for a moment. Andrew, forgive me for doubting you."

Andrew felt strangely embarrassed. He knew perfectly well that he had not moved from the chair, that he had not touched anything except Ellemir's fingertips, that Damon had not touched him at all, but he had the definite feeling that something profound and almost sexual had happened among all of them, including Callista, who was not there at all. "How much of what I felt was real?" he demanded.

Damon shrugged. "Define your terms. What's *real?* Everything and nothing. Oh, the images," he said, apparently picking up the texture of Andrew's embarrassment. "That. Let me put it this way. When the brain — or the mind — has an experience like nothing *else* it's ever experienced, it visualizes it in terms of familiar things. I lost contact for a few seconds — but I imagine you felt strong emotion."

"Yes," Andrew said, almost inaudibly.

"It was an unusual emotion, so your mind instantly associated it with a familiar but equally strong one, which just happened to be sexual. My own image is like walking a tightrope without falling off, and then finding something to hang on to, and brace myself with. But" — he grinned suddenly — "an awful lot of people think in sexual images, so don't worry about it. I'm used to it and so is anyone who's ever had to find their way around in direct *rapport.* Everybody has his own individual set of images; you'll soon recognize them like individual voices."

Ellemir said, almost in a murmur, "I kept hearing voices in different pitches, that suddenly slid in to close harmony and started singing to-

160

gether like an enormous choir."

Damon leaned over and touched her cheek lightly with his lips. "So that was the music I heard?" he murmured.

Andrew realized that somewhere in the back of his mind he too had heard something like far-off voices blending. Musical images, he thought a little wryly, were safer and less revealing than sexual ones. He looked tentatively at Ellemir, sounding out his own feelings, and found he was thinking on two levels at once. On one level he felt an intimacy with Ellemir, as if he had been her lover for a long time, a comprehensive good-will, a feeling of sympathy and protectiveness. On another level, even clearer, he was perfectly aware that this was a girl unfamiliar to him, that he had never touched more than her fingertips, and had no intention of ever doing any more than that and it confused him.

How can I feel this almost sexual acceptance of her, and at the same time have no sexual interest in her at all, as a person? Maybe Damon's right and I'm just visualizing unfamiliar feelings in familiar terms. Because I have that same sort of profound intimacy and acceptance toward Damon, *and that's* really *confusing and disturbing.* It gave him a headache.

Damon said, "I didn't see Callista, either, and I wasn't really in touch with her, but I could feel that Carr was." He sighed, with the weariness of physical fatigue, but his face was peaceful.

But the peaceful interlude was short-lived. Damon knew that, so far, Callista was well and safe. If anyone harmed her now, Andrew would know. But how long would she remain safe? If her captors had any idea that Callista had reached anyone outside, anyone who could lead rescuers to her — well, there was one obvious way to prevent that. Andrew couldn't reach her if she was dead. And that was so simple, and so obvious, that Damon's throat squeezed tight in panic. If they caught any hint of what he was trying to do, if they had the faintest notion that rescue was on the way, Callista might not live long enough to be rescued.

Why had they kept her alive this long? Again Damon reminded himself not to judge the cat-men by human standards. *We really know nothing of why they do anything.*

He rose, and swayed where he stood, knowing that after taxing, demanding telepathic work he needed food, sleep, and quiet. The night was far gone. The hideous need for haste beat at him. He braced himself to keep from falling and looked down at Ellemir and Andrew. *Now that things have begun moving again, we must be ready to move with them,* he thought. *If I'm going to act as Keeper, this is my responsibility — to keep them from panicking. I'm in charge, and I've got to look after them.*

"We all need food," he said, "and sleep. And we can't do a thing until we know how badly Dom Esteban is hurt. Everything, now, depends on that."

Chapter
EIGHT

When Damon came down into the Great Hall
the next morning, he found Eduin prowling
around in front of the doors, his face pale and
drawn. To Damon's question he nodded briefly.
"Caradoc's doing well enough, Lord Damon.
But the Lord Istvan —"

That told Damon all he needed to know.
Esteban Lanart had awakened — and was still
unable to move. So that was *that.* Damon felt a
sickening sensation as if he stood on quicksand.
What now? *What now?*

Then it was up to him. He realized, hardening
his jaw, that he had really known this all along.
From the moment of premonition (*You will see
him sooner than you think and it will not be well for
any of you*) he had known that in the end it would
be his task. He was still not sure how, but at least
he knew he could not let the burden slide onto
the stronger shoulders of his kinsman.

"Does he know, Eduin?"

Eduin's hawklike face twisted in a grimace of
compassion and he said briefly, "Do you think
anyone'd need to *tell* him? Aye. He knows."

And if he didn't, he'd know the minute he saw me. Damon began to push aside the doors to enter, but Eduin gripped his arm.

"Can't you do for his wound what you did for Caradoc's, Lord Damon?"

Pityingly, Damon shook his head. "I'm no miracle worker. To stop the flow of blood is nothing. That done, Caradoc would heal. I healed nothing; I did only what Caradoc's wound would have done of itself if anyone could have reached it. But if the spinal nerve is severed — no power on this world could repair it."

Eduin's eyes closed briefly. "That I feared," he said. "Lord Damon! Is there news of the Lady Callista?"

"We know she is safe and well, at this moment," Damon said, "but there is need for haste. So I must see Dom Esteban at once, and make plans."

He pushed the door open. Ellemir was kneeling by her father's bedside; the other wounded men had evidently been moved out to the Guardroom, except for Caradoc, who lay under blankets far at the back of the Hall, and seemed fast asleep. Esteban Lanart lay flat, his heavy body immobilized in sandbags so that he could not turn from side to side. Ellemir was feeding him, not very expertly, with a child's spoon. He was a tall, heavy, red-faced man, with the strongly aquiline features of all his clan, his long sideburns and bushy eyebrows graying but his beard still brilliantly red. He looked angry and incongruous with drops of gruel in his beard; his fierce eyes moved to Damon.

"Good morning, kinsman," Damon said.

Dom Esteban retorted, "Good, you say! When I lie here like a tree struck by lightning and my daughter — my daughter —" He raised a clenched fist in rage, struck the spoon, upset more of the gruel, and snarled, "Take that filthy stuff away! It's not my belly that's paralyzed, girl!" He saw her stricken face and moved his hand clumsily to pat her arm. "Sorry, *chiya*. I've cause enough for anger. But get me something decent to eat, not that baby-food!"

Ellemir raised helpless eyes to the healer-woman who stood by; she shrugged, and Damon said, "Give him anything he wants, Ellemir, unless he's feverish."

The girl rose and went out, and Damon came to the bedside. It seemed inconceivable that Dom Esteban would never again rise from that bed. That harsh face should not lie on a pillow, that powerful body should be up and moving about in its usual brisk military way.

"I won't ask you how you feel, kinsman," Damon said. "But are you in much pain now?"

"Almost none, strange as it seems," said the wounded man. "Such a little, little wound to lay me low! Hardly more than a scratch. And yet —" His teeth clenched in his lip. "I've been told I'll never walk again." His gray eyes sought out Damon's, in an agony of pleading so great that the younger man was embarrassed. "Is it true?

165

Or is the woman as much a fool as she seems?"

Damon bent his head and did not answer. After a moment the older man moved his head in weary resignation. "Tragedy stalks our family. Coryn dead before his fifteenth year, and Callista, Callista — so I must seek help, humbly, as befits a cripple, from strangers. I have no one of my own blood to help me."

Damon knelt on one knee beside the old man. He said deliberately, "The gods forbid you should seek among strangers. I claim that right — father-in-law."

The bushy eyebrows went up, almost into the hairline. At last Dom Esteban said, "So the wind blows from that quarter? I had other plans for Ellemir, but —" A brief pause, then, "Nothing goes, I believe, as we plan it, in this imperfect world. Be it so, then. But the road will be no easy one, even if you can find Callista. Ellemir has told me something — a confused tale of Callista and a stranger, a Terran, who has somehow gained *rapport* with her and has offered his sword, or his services, or some such thing. He must talk of it with you, whoever he is, although it seems strange that one of the Terranan should show proper reverence for a Keeper." He scowled fiercely. "Curse those beasts! Damon, what has been happening in these hills? Until a few seasons ago the cat-men were timid folk who lived in the hills, and no one thought them wiser than the little people of the trees! Then, as if some evil god had come among them, they attack us like

166

fiends, they stir up the Dry Towns against us — and lands where our people have lived for generations lie under some darkness as if bewitched. I'm a practical man, Damon, and I don't believe in bewitchments! And now they come invisible out of the air, like wizards from some old fairy tale."

"All too real, I fear," Damon said, and knew his face was grim. "I met them, crossing the darkening lands, and only too late did I realize that I could have made them visible with my starstone." His hand sought the leather pouch about his throat. "They slaughtered my men. Eduin said you saved them, that almost alone you cut your way out of the ambush. How — ?" Damon felt suddenly awkward.

Dom Esteban lifted the long, squarish swordsman's hand from the bed and looked at it, as if puzzled. "I hardly know," he said slowly, looking at his hand and moving the fingers back and forth, turning it to look at the palm, and then back again. "I must have heard the other sword in the air —" He hesitated and an odd note of wonder crept into his voice as he spoke again. "But I didn't. Not till I had my sword out and up to guard." He blinked, puzzled. "It's like that sometimes. It's happened before. You suddenly turn, and block, and there's an attack coming that you'd never have seen unless you'd found yourself guarding it." He laughed again, raucously. "Merciful Avarra! Listen to the old man bragging." Suddenly the fingers knotted into fists. The arm trembled with anger. "Boast? Why not? What else can a cripple do?"

From the greatest swordsman in the Domains to a helpless invalid — horrible! And yet, Damon thought reluctantly, there was an element of justice in it. Dom Esteban had never been tolerant of the slightest physical weakness in anyone else. It had been in proving his courage to his father, climbing the heights he feared, that Coryn had fallen to his death. . . .

"Zandru's hells," the old man said after a moment. "The way my joints have stiffened, these last three winters, the bone-aches would have done it in another year or so, anyway. Better to have one last terrific fight."

"It won't be forgotten in a hurry," Damon said, and turned quickly away so the old man would not see the pity in his eyes. "Zandru's hells, how we could use your sword now against the accursed cat-men!"

The old man laughed mirthlessly. "My sword? That's easy — take it and welcome," he said with a bitter grimace meant to be a grin. "Afraid you'll have to use it yourself, though. I can't go along and help."

Damon caught the unspoken contempt — *There's no sword ever forged could make a swordsman of you* — but at the moment he felt no anger. Dom Esteban's only remaining weapon was his tongue. Anyway, Damon had never prided himself on his skill at arms.

Ellemir was returning with a tray of solid food

for her father; she set it down beside the bed and began cutting up the meat. Dom Esteban said, "Just what are your plans, Damon? *You're* not planning to go up against the cat-men?"

He said quietly, "I see no alternative, Father-in-law."

"It will take an army to wipe them out, Damon."

"Time enough for that next year," Damon said. "Just now our first problem is to get Callista out of their hands, and for that we have no time to raise an army. What's more, if we came up against them with an army, their first move would be to kill her. Time presses. Now that we know where she is —"

Dom Esteban stared, forgetting to chew a mouthful of meat and gravy. He swallowed, choked a little, gestured to Ellemir for a drink, and said, "You know. Just how did you manage that?"

"The Terranan," said Damon quietly. "No, I don't know how it happened either. I never knew any of the strangers had anything like our *laran*. But he has it, and he is in contact with Callista."

"I don't doubt it," Esteban said. "I met some of them in Thendara when they negotiated to build the Trade City. They are more like us. I heard a story that Terra and Darkover are of common stock, far back in history. They rarely leave their city, though. How did this one come here?"

"I will send for him and you can hear it from

his own lips," said Ellemir. She beckoned a servant and gave the message, and after a little while Andrew Carr came into the Great Hall. Damon, watching the Earthman bowing to Dom Esteban, thought that at least these people were no savages.

Prompted by Damon, Carr gave a brief account of how he had come into contact with Callista. Esteban looked grave and thoughtful.

"I cannot say that I approve of this," he said. "For a Keeper to make such close contact with a stranger from outside her own caste is unheard-of, and scandalous. In the old days of the Domains, wars were fought on Darkover for less than this. But times change, whether we like the changes or not, and perhaps as things stand now it is more important to save her from the cat-men than from the disgrace of such a *rapport*."

"Disgrace?" Andrew Carr said, flushing deeply. "I mean her no harm or dishonor, sir. I wish her nothing but the best, and I have offered to risk my life to set her free."

"Why?" Esteban asked curtly. "She can be nothing to you, man; a Keeper is pledged a virgin."

Damon hoped Carr would have sense enough not to say anything about his own emotional attachment to Callista; but not trusting Andrew to hold his tongue, he said, "Dom Esteban, he has already risked his life to make contact with her; for a man of his age, untrained, to work through a starstone is no light matter." He scowled at Andrew, trying to convey "Shut up, let well enough alone."

In any case, Dom Esteban, whether from pain or worry, did not pursue the topic, but turned to Damon. "You know, then, where Callista is?"

"We have reason to believe she is in the caves of Corresanti," Damon said, "and Andrew can lead us to her."

Dom Esteban snorted. "There's a lot of countryside between here and Corresanti, and all of it chock full of cat-men, and blasted villages," he said. "It lies half a day's ride into the darkening lands."

"That can't be helped," Damon said. "You managed to get through them, which proves it can be done. At least they cannot come on us veiled by invisibility, while I have my starstone."

Esteban thought about that; nodded slowly. "I had forgotten you were Tower-trained," he said. "What about the Earthman? Will he come with you?"

Andrew said, "I'm going. I seem to be the only link to Callista. Besides, I swore to her that I would rescue her."

Damon shook his head. "No, Andrew. No, my friend. Just *because* you are the only link with Callista, we dare not risk you. If you were killed, even accidentally, we might never make our way to her, or recover only her dead body, too late. You stay at Armida, and maintain contact with me, through the starstone."

Stubbornly, Carr shook his head. "Look, I'm

171

going," he said. "I'm a lot bigger and tougher than you think. I've knocked around on half a dozen worlds. I can take care of myself, Damon. Hell, man, I'd make two of *you!*"

Damon sighed, and thought, *Maybe he can; he got here through the blizzard. I couldn't have done that well if I were lost on a strange world.* "Possibly you're right," he said. "How good are you with a sword?"

Damon saw the faint surprise and hesitation in the Earthman's face. "I don't know. My people don't use them except for sport. I could learn, though. I learn fast."

Damon raised his eyebrows. "It's not that easy," he said. *His people use swords only for sport? How do they defend themselves, then? Knives, like the Dry-Towners, or fists? If so, they may be stronger than we are. Or have the Terrans gone beyond the Compact, and banned all weapons that can kill at all?*

He said, "Eduin," and the big Guardsman, lounging near the door, sprang to attention. *"Vai dom?"*

"Step over to the armory, and get a couple of practice swords."

After a moment Eduin returned, bearing two of the wood-and-leather weapons used for training in swordsmanship. Damon took one in his hand, extended the other to Carr. The Earthman looked curiously at the long blunt stick of springy wood, with braided leather covering the edge and tip, then experimentally gripped it in

172

his palm. Damon, frowning at the unpracticed grip, asked bluntly, "Have you ever touched a sword before in your life?"

"A little fencing for sport. I'm no champion."

I can well believe that, Damon thought, slipping on the leather headpiece. He looked at Carr over his right shoulder through the grillwork that protected his face: the practice swords bent easily enough that there was not much danger of damaging a bone or an internal organ, but eyes and teeth were more vulnerable. Carr faced him straight on. *Chest exposed,* Damon thought, *and he handles the thing as if he were poking the fire.*

Andrew stepped forward; Damon lifted his sword only slightly, brushing the weapon aside. As the big man went off balance, the leather tip caught Carr in the chest. Then Damon relaxed, lowering the tip to the floor. He slowly shook his head. He said, "You see, my friend? And I'm no swordsman. I wouldn't last half a dozen strokes against anyone even halfway competent; Dom Esteban, or Eduin here, would have had the sword out of my hand before I got it up —"

"I'm sure I could learn," Carr protested stubbornly.

"Not in time," Damon said. "Believe me. Andrew, I began to train with these swords before I was eight years old. Most lads begin at least a year before that. You're strong — I can see that. You're even fairly fast on your feet. But we couldn't even teach you enough, in a week, to keep you from getting killed. And we haven't got a week. We haven't even got a day. Forget it, Andrew. You've got something more important to do than carrying a sword."

"And do you think *you're* going to lead a party of swordsmen against the cat-people?" Dom Esteban asked sardonically. "Eduin here could do to you what you did to the Earthman, in seconds."

Damon looked around at the man lying motionless. Esteban had motioned the tray of food away, and was watching them fixedly, his eyes bright with something like anger. He said, "Show some sense, Damon. I kept you in the Guards because the men like you and you're a good organizer and administrator. But this is a job for a master swordsman. Are you so blind to facts that you think you could go up against swordsmen who could cut down the whole castle Guard here at Armida and steal Callista right out of her bed? Am I marrying my daughter to a fool?"

Ellemir said in a rage, "Father, how dare you! You cannot talk like that to Damon!"

Damon motioned to her to be quiet. He faced the older man straightforwardly, and said, "I know that, kinsman. I probably know more about my own deficiencies than you do. Just the same, no man can do more than his best, and this is my right. I am now Callista's closest kinsman, except for Domenic, and he is not yet seventeen."

Esteban smiled grimly. He said, "Well, my son, I admire your spirit; I wish you had the skill to go

174

with it." He raised his fists and beat them against the pillow, in a fit of fury. "Zandru's hells! Here I lie, broken-down and useless as Durraman's donkey, and all my skill and all my knowledge —" The fit subsided at last and he said, his voice weaker than before, "If I had time to teach you, you're not so hopeless — but there's no time, no time. You say with your starstone you can throw off their accursed illusion of invisibility?"

Damon nodded. Eduin came forward to the bedside and knelt there. He said, "Lord Istvan. I owe the Lord Damon a life. Let me go with them to Corresanti."

Damon said, deeply moved, "You're wounded, man. And you've been through one battle."

"All the same," Eduin protested, "you have said my skill with a sword is greater than your own. Let me go to guard you, Lord Damon; your task is to bear the starstone."

"Merciful Avarra," Dom Esteban said almost under his breath, "*that* is the answer!"

"I will gladly have your company and your sword, if you are able," Damon said, laying his hand on Eduin's shoulder. In his sensitized state he was overwhelmingly aware of the man's out-pouring of loyalty and gratitude, and he felt almost abashed by it. "But you owe your service to the Lord Esteban; it is for him to give you leave to go with me."

Both men turned to Esteban, who lay motion-less; his eyes were closed and his brow knitted as if deep in thought. For a moment Damon wondered if they had exhausted the wounded man too much, but he could feel that beneath the closed eyes there was some very active thinking going on. Esteban's eyes suddenly flew open.

"Just how good are you with that starstone, Damon?" he asked. "I know you have *laran*, you spent years in the Tower, but didn't Leonie kick you out again? If it was for incompetence, this won't work, but —"

"It wasn't for incompetence," Damon said quietly. "Leonie did not complain of my skill, only that I was too sensitive, and my health, she felt, would suffer."

"Look me in the eye. Is that truth or vanity, Damon?"

There were times, Damon thought, when he positively detested the brutal old man. He met Esteban's eyes without flinching and said, "As I remember, *you* have enough *laran* to find out for yourself."

Esteban's lips flicked in that mirthless grin again. He said, "From somewhere, you've gotten courage enough to stand up to me, kinsman, and that's a good sign. As a lad you were afraid of me. Is it only because I'll never move out of this bed again that you've got courage to confront me now?" He returned Damon's gaze for an instant — a harsh touch like a firm grip — and then said tersely, "My apology for doubting you, kinsman, but this is too important to spare anyone's feelings, even my own. Do you think I like confronting the fact that someone else will rescue my favorite daughter? Just the same. You are skilled with a starstone. Have you ever heard the story of Regis the Fifth? The Hasturs were kings in those days; it was before the crown passed into the Elhalyn line."

Damon frowned, searching in memory of old legends. "He lost a leg in the battle of Dammerung Pass — ?"

"No," said Dom Esteban, "he lost a leg by treachery, when he was set on in his bed by assassins; so that he could not fight in a duel and would forfeit a good half of the Hastur lands. Yet he sent his brother Rafael to the battle, and Rafael, who was a monkish man with little knowledge of swordplay, nevertheless fought in single combat with seven men and killed them all. To this day Castle Hastur stands in Hastur hands at the edge of the mountains. And this he could do because, as Regis lay in his bed not yet able to rise and hobble about on crutches, he made contact through his brother's starstone with his sword, and the monkish Rafael bore the sword of Regis into the fight, wielding it with all of Regis' skill."

"A fairy tale," said Damon, but he felt a strange prickle go up and down his spine.

Dom Esteban moved his head as much as he could for the sandbags and said vehemently, "By the honor of the Alton Domain, Damon, it is no fairy tale. The skill was known in the old times, but in these days few of the Comyn have the strength or the wish to dare so much. In these days the starstones are left mostly to women. Yet, if I thought you had the skills of our fathers with such a stone —"

With a slow prickle of wonder, Damon realized what Dom Esteban was suggesting. He said, "But —"

"Are you afraid? Do you think you could stand the touch of the Alton Gift?" Dom Esteban demanded. "If it enabled you to fight your way through the cat-men with my own skill?"

Damon shut his eyes. He said honestly, "I'd have to think about it. It wouldn't be easy."

Yet — might it be Callista's one chance?

Dom Esteban was the only living man to cut his way out of a cat-man ambush. He himself had run like a rabbit from them, leaving his men to die. He had to be sure about this. He knew it was the kind of decision no one else could make for him. For a moment no one else in the room existed but Esteban and himself.

He stepped close to the bed and looked down at the prostrate man. "If I refuse, kinsman, it is not because I am afraid, but because I doubt your power to do this, sick and wounded as you are. I knew not that you had the Alton Gift, bred true."

"Oh, yes, I have it," said Esteban, staring up with a fearful intensity, "but in such days as I am living in, I always believed, I needed no gift other than my own strength and skill with weapons. Where do you suppose Callista got it in such measure that she was chosen from all the girls of the Domains to be Keeper? The Alton Gift is the ability to force *rapport,* and I had some training in my own youth. Try me, if you will."

Ellemir came and slid her hand into Damon's. She said, "Father, you can't do this dreadful thing."

"Dreadful? Why, my girl?"

"It's against the strongest law of the Comyn: that no man may dominate another's mind and soul."

"Who said anything about his mind and soul?" asked the old man, his gray bushy eyebrows crawling up like giant caterpillars to his hairline. "It's his sword-arm and reflexes I'm interested in dominating, and I *can* do it. And I'll do it by his free will and consent, or not at all." He began to reach out, winced, and lay still between the sand-bags. "It's your choice, Damon."

Andrew looked pale and worried; Damon himself felt much the same way, and Ellemir's hand, tucked in his, was trembling. He said slowly, "If it's Callista's best chance, I'd agree to more than that. If you are strong enough, Lord Esteban."

"If my damned useless legs would only move, I've *fought* with worse wounds than this," Dom Esteban said. "Take the practice sword. Eduin, you take the other."

Damon slipped on the basketwork headpiece, turned his right side to Eduin. The Guardsman saluted, standing very casually, legs apart, sword-tip resting on the ground. Damon felt a

179

sharp spasm of fear.

Not that Eduin could hurt me much with these wooden swords, not that I care so much for a few bumps and bruises. But all my life that damnable old man has been baiting me about my lack of skill. To make a fool of myself before Ellemir . . . to let him humiliate me once again. . . .

Esteban said in a strange, faraway voice, "Your starstone is insulated, Damon. Uncover it."

Damon fumbled with the leather pouch, drew it off, letting the warm heaviness of the matrix jewel rest against the base of his throat. He gave the pouch to Ellemir to hold, and the quick brush of her warm fingers against his was a reassurance.

Esteban said, "Stand back, Ellemir. And you too, Terranan. By the door, and see that no servants come in here. They can't do much harm with the practice foils, but even so —"

They withdrew slowly, and the two men faced one another, the heavy wooden swords in hand, circling slowly. Damon was faintly conscious of the harsh grip-touch that was Dom Esteban's (*What did I tell Andrew, you get to recognize people by their images as well as by their voices?*) and felt a strange droning in his ears, a sense of harsh pressure. He saw Eduin's sword come up, and before he knew what he was doing, he felt the flexing of his own knees, his arm moving without his knowledge in a quick whirling stroke. He heard the rapid-fire *whack! whack! whack!* of wood-and-leather clashing, then saw an incongruous

180

whirl of images: Eduin's astonished face, with its seamed raw wound; Andrew's flare of amazement; his own arm coming up and a rapid backward step and feint; Eduin's sword flying out of his hand and across the room, landing almost at Andrew Carr's feet. The Earthman bent and picked it up as the droning suddenly receded from Damon's head.

Esteban said quietly, "Now do you believe me, kinsman? Have you ever been able to touch Eduin before, let alone disarm him?"

Damon realized that he was breathing fast and his heart beating like a smith's hammer at the forge. He thought, *I never moved that fast in my life,* and felt a mingled fear and resentment. *Someone else's hand, someone else's mind . . . in control . . . control of my very body.*

And yet — To get back at the damned cat-things who killed his Guardsmen, Dom Esteban would have been the logical choice to lead swordsmen against them. And he would if he could.

Damon had never especially wanted to be a swordsman. It wasn't his game. Just the same, he owed the cat-men something. His men were relying on him, and he'd left them to die. And Reidel had been his friend. If with Dom Esteban's help he could do it, did he have the right to refuse?

Esteban was lying quite still, passive between his sandbags, just flexing and unflexing his fingers thoughtfully. He did not speak, only met

Damon's eyes with a look of triumph.

Damon thought, *Damn the man, he's enjoying this. But after all, why shouldn't he? He's proved to himself that he's not completely useless, after all.*

He put down the practice sword. From the naked jewel against his throat he was picking up flashing impressions, wonder and terror from Eduin, a sort of bemusement from Andrew, dismay from Ellemir. He tried to shut them all out, and went toward the bed again.

He said slowly, steadily — but he had to force the words out — "I agree, then, kinsman. When can we start?"

Chapter
NINE

They started later that day, near to high noon, and Andrew, watching them ride away from the roof of Armida, thought they were a small party to go up against an army of nonhumans. He said so to Ellemir, who stood beside him wrapped to the earlobes in a heavy plaid shawl of green and blue. She shook her head, saying in an odd far-away voice, "Force alone wouldn't get them through. Damon has the only weapon that matters — the starstone."

"It looks to me like he'll be doing some fairly tough fighting — or your father will," Andrew said.

Ellemir answered, "Not really. That will just — if he's lucky — keep him from getting killed. But swordsmen have failed, before this, to get into the darkening lands. The cat-men know it, too. I am sure they took Callista in the hope of capturing her starstone as well. The cat-people who are using a matrix unlawfully must have discovered that she was here — in a general way one matrix-user can spy out another — and hoped to gain her stone. Perhaps they even hoped they could force her to use it against us. Men would have known better — they would have known that any Keeper would die first. But the cat-people are apparently just beginning to learn about these things — which is why there is still some hope."

Andrew was thinking, grimly, that was lucky; if they had known more about Keepers, the cat-people would not have kidnapped Callista, but simply left her lying with her throat cut, in her bed. He saw from Ellemir's grimace of horror that she had followed his thoughts.

The woman said in a low voice, "Damon blames himself for running away and leaving his men to be slaughtered. But it was the right thing to do. If they had captured him, *and his starstone* — alive —"

"I thought no one could use another's stone except under very special circumstances."

"Not without hurting its owner terribly. But do you think the cat-men would have hesitated to do that?" she asked, almost with contempt, and was silent.

The riders had virtually disappeared now, only three small dots on the horizon: Damon and two swordsmen of the guard.

Andrew thought bitterly, *I should have been with them. Rescuing Callista is my job; instead I sit here at Armida, no more use than Dom Esteban. Less. He's fighting along with them.*

He had wanted to go. He had thought until the last that he would ride with them, that he would be needed to guide them to Callista, at least when they got inside the caves. After all, he was the only one who could reach her. Damon, even with his starstone, couldn't. But Damon had absolutely refused.

"Andrew, no, it's impossible. The best bodyguard in the world wouldn't be able to ensure you against getting killed accidentally. You are absolutely helpless to defend yourself, let alone help anyone else. It's not your fault, my friend, but all our energies have to go to getting inside the caves and getting Callista out. The spare minute we might take to defend you might make the difference between getting out alive — or not. And — let me remind you — if we get killed," he said, his lips tightening, "someone else can try. If *you* get killed, Callista will die inside the caves, from starvation, or ill-treatment, or with a knife in her throat when they discover she's no good to them." Damon had laid his hand on Andrew's shoulder, regretfully. "Believe me, I know how you feel. But this is the only way."

"And how will you find her without me there? You can't, even with your starstone; you just said so!"

"With Callista's starstone," Damon said. "*You* have access to the overworld. And you can reach me, too. Once I am inside the caves, you can lead us to her through the starstone."

Andrew still wasn't sure how that would be done. He had, in spite of yesterday's demonstration, only the foggiest notion of *how* it worked. He had *seen* it work, he had *felt* it work, but twenty-eight years of not believing in such things weren't wiped away in twenty-eight hours.

At his side, on the parapet, Ellemir shivered and said, "They're gone. There's no sense standing out here in the cold." She turned and went in through the doorway that led into the upper corridor of Armida, and slowly, Carr followed.

He knew Damon was right — or more accurately, he had faith that Damon knew what he was doing — but it was still galling. For days now, ever since he had realized that if he lived through the storm, somehow he would find Callista and rescue her, he had sustained himself with a mental picture of Callista, alone in the darkness of her prison, of himself coming to her side and sweeping her up in his arms, and carrying her away. . . . *Some damn romantic dream,* he thought sourly. *Where's the white horse to carry her away?*

He had never envisioned a world where men took swords seriously. For him a sword was either something to look at on the wall of a museum, or something to play with for exercise. He had wished for a gun or a blaster — *that* would make short work of a cat-man, he'd bet — but when he had said so, Damon had looked at him with as much horror as if he'd suggested gangrape, cannibalism, and genocide, and mentioned something called the Compact. Before signing his contract with the Empire on Cottman IV, Andrew *had* fuzzily noted that they did have something there called the Compact, which as near as he could understand — he hadn't paid much attention to it, you never paid much attention to technicalities of native culture — forbade any lethal weapons which didn't bring the user within an equal risk of being killed in return. Damon had spoken of it, saying it had been universally accepted on Darkover, which seemed to be his name for the planet, for either a few hundred years or a few thousand. Andrew wasn't sure which; his command of the language was improving, but still wasn't perfect. So guns were definitely out, although swordplay had become a fine art.

No wonder they start training their kids in fighting before they're out of short pants. He wondered, in view of the ghastly cold weather on this planet, if children ever wore short pants at all, and cut off the thought with impatience. He went into the guest-room they had assigned him earlier and walked to the window, drawing aside the curtain to see if he could still catch a glimpse of Damon's party disappearing. But evidently they had ridden away past the crest of the hill.

Andrew lay down on the bed, hands tucked behind his neck. He supposed sooner or later he should go down and say a few polite words to his host. He didn't much like Dom Esteban; the man had tried hard to humiliate Damon, but the man was an invalid, and his host. Also, he felt some sense of obligation toward Ellemir. He didn't know what he could say to her, torn as she was between fear for Callista, fear for Damon, and anxiety about her father. But if he could do anything, or say anything, to let her know he shared her anxiety, he ought to do it.

Callista, Callista, he thought, *it's some world you brought me into.* Nevertheless, he felt a curious acceptance of what he would find here.

Callista's starstone around his neck felt reassuringly warm, like a live thing. *It's like touching Callista herself,* he thought, *the nearest to touching her that I've ever come.* Even through the silk insulation, there was an intimacy in the touch against his throat. He wondered where she was, if it was well with her, if she was crying alone in the darkness?

Damon seemed to think I could reach her through the stone, Andrew thought, and he drew it from his shirt front. The grayish silk envelope in which it was wrapped protected it from a careless touch. Carefully, mindful of Damon's warning, he unwrapped it with infinite caution, and a curious sense of hesitation. *It's almost as if I were undressing Callista,* he thought with a tender embarrassment, and at the same time he was ready to explode with hysterical laughter at the incongruity of the idea.

As he cradled the stone in his palm, he suddenly saw her close beside him. She was lying on her side, her lovely hair tangled — he could see her in a strange bluish light quite unlike the dim red sunlight in the room — and her face blotched and swollen as if she had been crying again. Quite without surprise, she opened her eyes and looked at him.

"Andrew, is it you? I had wondered why you had not come to me before," she said softly, and smiled.

"Damon is on his way to you," Andrew said, and the surge of resentment that he was not with them, that *he* would not be the one to find her, boiled over. He tried to conceal it from her and realized too late that he could not, that in this kind of close touching of minds no thought could be concealed.

She said very tenderly, "You must not be jealous of Damon; he has been as a brother to me since we were children."

Andrew felt ashamed of his own jealousy. *It's no good to pretend not to be jealous, I'll just have to get beyond thoughts like that.* He tried to remember how much he had liked Damon, how close he had felt to him for a little while, that in the deepest way of all he was grateful to Damon for doing what he himself couldn't, and he saw Callista smiling gently at him. He sensed somehow that he had overcome one of the first major barriers to acceptance on their own terms as one of themselves in a telepath culture, that because of this he was somehow less of an alien to Callista than he had been before.

She said, "You can come to me in the overworld now."

He looked at her helplessly. "I don't know how."

"Take the stone and look into it," she said. "I can see it, you know. I can see it like a light in the darkness. But you must not come to me *here*, where my body is. If my captors should see you, they might kill me to keep me from being rescued. I will come to you." Abruptly, without transition, the girl lying wearily on her side in the dark cave was standing before him at the foot of the bed. "Now," she said. "Simply leave your solid body behind; step out of it."

Andrew focused on the stone, fighting back the faint, crawling inner nausea, the perceptible surge of terror. Callista held out her hand to him, and suddenly, with a strange, tingling sensation, he was standing upright (he had not moved at all, he thought), and below him he could see his body, clad in the heavy unfamiliar garments Damon had given him, lying motionless on the bed, the stone between his hands.

He reached out his hand on the overworld level, and for the first time touched Callista's. It felt faint, and ethereal, hardly a physical touch at all, but it *was* a touch, he could *feel* it, and he saw from Callista's face that she felt it, too.

She whispered, "Yes, you are real, you are here. Oh, Andrew, Andrew —" For an instant she let herself fall against him. It was like embracing a shadow, but still, for an instant, he felt her light weight against him, felt the warmth and fragrance of her body in his arms, the wispy feel of her hair. He wanted to crush her in his arms and cover her with kisses, but something in her

190

— a faint sense of hesitation, a drawing away — kept him from acting on his impulse.

I'm not even supposed to think about a Keeper. They're sacrosanct. Untouchable.

She raised her shadowy fingers to lay them gently against his cheek. She said very gently, "There will be time enough to think about all that later, when I am with you — really with you, really close to you."

"Callista. You know I love you," he said hesitantly, and her mouth trembled.

"I know, and it is strange to me, and I suppose under any other conditions it would be frightening to me. But you have come to me when I was so terribly alone, and fearing death, or torment, or ravishment. Men have desired me before," she said very simply, "and of course I have been taught, in ways I couldn't even begin to explain to you, not to respond to them in any way, even in fancy. With some men, it has made me feel — feel sick, as if insects were crawling on my body. But there have been a few that I have almost wished — wished, as I wish now with you — that I knew how to respond to their desire; even, perhaps, that I knew how to desire them in return. Can you understand this at all?"

"Not really," Andrew said slowly, "but I'll try to understand what you're feeling. I can't help how I feel, Callista, but I'll try not to feel anything you don't want me to." To a telepath girl, he was thinking, a lustful thought must have some of the quality of a rape. Was that why it was

191

rude to look at a young woman here? To protect them against one's thoughts?

"But I want you to," Callista said shyly. "I'm not sure what it would feel like to — to love anyone. But I want you to go on thinking about me. It makes me feel less lonely somehow. Alone in the dark, I feel as if I am not real, even to myself."

Andrew felt an infinite tenderness. Poor child; brainwashed and conditioned against any emotion, what had they made of her? If only he could do something, anything to comfort her. . . . He felt so damned helpless, miles and miles away from her, and Callista alone in the dark and frightened. He whispered to her, "Keep up your courage, my darling. We'll have you out of there soon," and as the words escaped him he found himself back in his body, lying on the bed, feeling sick and faint and somehow drained. But at least he knew Callista was alive, and well — as well as she could possibly be, he amended — until Damon got her out of there.

He lay quiet for a moment, resting. Evidently telepathic work was a lot more strenuous than physical activity; he felt about like he had when he'd been fighting his way through the blizzard.

Fighting. But Damon was doing the real fighting. Somewhere out there, Damon had the really serious task, fighting his way through the cat-men — and from what he'd seen downstairs, when Dom Esteban's party had dragged themselves home, wounded and broken, the cat-men were damned formidable antagonists.

Damon had told him that it was for him to lead them to Callista, once Damon was inside the caves. He supposed he could do that, now that he knew how to step outside his body — what Callista had first called his "solid" body — and into the overworld. Then a frightening thought struck him.

Callista was in some level of the overworld where she could not reach, or even see, Damon, or Ellemir, or any of her friends. He, Carr, could reach her, somehow; but did that mean that he was on *her* part of the overworld, the only one the cat-men had left open to Callista? If that was true, then *he* couldn't reach Damon either! And how in *hell* — in that case — could he lead Damon anywhere?

Once the thought had come into his mind it would not be dispelled. *Could* he reach Damon? Even through the starstone? Or would he find himself, like Callista, wandering like a ghost in the overworld, unable to reach any familiar human face?

Nonsense. Damon knew what he was doing. They had been in contact, last night, through the stones. (Again the memory of that curiously intimate moment of fusion warmed and disturbed him.)

Just the same . . . the doubt lingered, would not be chased away. Finally he realized there was only one way to be sure, and once again he drew forth the starstone from its silk envelope. This time, he did not attempt to physically move out of his body into the overworld, but concentrated, with all his strength, on Damon, repeating his name.

The stone clouded. Again the curious creeping sickness (Would he ever get past that stage? Would he ever be free of it?) surged up and he struggled for control, trying to focus his thoughts on Damon. Deep in the depths of the blue stone — as he had seen Callista's face, so long ago now in the Trade City — he saw tiny figures, like riders, and he knew that he saw Damon's party, the swirling cloak of green-gold, which Damon had told him were the colors of the Ridenow family, the two tall riders on either side. Over them, like a menace, hovered a dark cloud, a dimness, and a voice, not his own, whispered in Andrew's thoughts: *The edge of the darkening lands.* Then there was a curious flare and touch, and Andrew felt himself merging with another mind — he *was* Damon. . . .

Damon's body sat his horse with careless, automatic skill; no one who did not know him well would have realized that his body was empty of consciousness, that Damon himself rode somewhere *above*, his mind sweeping over the land before him, seeking, seeking.

The shadow rose before him, a thick darkness to his mind as it had been to his eyes, and again he felt the memory of fear, the apprehension which he had felt on leading his men into ambush unawares. . . . *Is this fear for now, or a memory of that fear?* Briefly, dropping back into his body, he felt Dom Esteban's sword, which lay loosely held in his right hand, twitch slightly, and knew he must control himself and react only to real dangers. It was Dom Esteban's sword, rather than Damon's own, because, as Dom Esteban put it, "I have carried it in a hundred battles. No other sword would come so ready to my hand. It knows my ways and my will." Damon had carried out the old man's wishes, remembering how the silver butterfly Callista wore in her hair carried the mental imprint of *her* personality. How much more, then, a sword on which Dom Esteban had depended for his very life, for over fifty years spent in battles, feuds, raiding parties?

In the hilt of the sword, Damon had set one of the small, unkeyed first-level matrixes which he had dismissed, at first, as being only fit to fasten buttons; small as it was, it would resonate in harmony with his own starstone and allow Dom Esteban to maintain contact not only with the energy-nets of his muscles and nerve centers, but with the hilt of his sword.

Spell sword, he thought, half derisively. But the history of Darkover was full of such weapons. There was the legendary Sword of Aldones in the chapel at Hali, a weapon so ancient — and so fearful — that no one alive knew how to wield it. There was the Sword of Hastur, in Castle Hastur, of which it was said that if any man drew it save in defense of the honor of the Hasturs it would blast his hand as if with fire. And that in turn reminded him of the Lady Mirella, whose body and hands had been burned and blackened as if with fire. . . .

His hand trembled faintly on the hilt of Dom Esteban's sword. Well, he was as well prepared for such a battle as any living man could be; Tower-trained, strong enough that Leonie had said that as a woman he would have been a Keeper. And as for the rest — well, he was riding in defense of his own kinswoman, taking up a duty for his father-in-law-to-be, and thus safeguarding the honor of his future wife's family.

And as for being a virgin, Damon thought wryly, *I'm not, but I'm as nearly chaste as any adult male my age could be. I didn't even bed Ellemir, although Evanda the Fair knows that I would have liked to.* To himself he recited the Creed of Chastity taught him at Nevarsin Monastery, where he had been schooled, like many sons of the Seven Domains, in childhood. The creed was adhered to by men working in the Tower Circles: never to lay hands on any unwilling woman, to look never with lewd thoughts on child or pledged virgin, to spend oneself never on such women as are common to all.

Well, I learned it so thoroughly in the Tower that I never unlearned it, and if it makes it safer for me on what is, basically, work for a Keeper — well, so much the better for me and so much the worse for the cat-men, Zandru seize them for his coldest hell!

He dropped back into his body, opened his eyes, and watched the land ahead of him. Then, carefully and slowly, he raised his consciousness again, leaving his body to react with long habit to the motion of the horse. He used the link of those open, staring eyes to send himself out over the physical landscape ahead, still brooding beneath that dark mist.

It was as darker clots of blackness just at the edge of that shadow that he saw them first; then the fine web of force that bound them to some other power, hidden in a depth of shadow that neither his eyes nor the power of the starstone could yet pierce.

Then he could see the furred bodies that those forces hid, crouched silent and motionless among little shrubs which could hardly have hidden them, visible.

Cats. Stalking mice. And we're the mice. He could see his own little group of men, moving steadily toward that ambush. He began to lower himself toward his body again. *Change their route. Avoid that ambush.*

But no. He blinked, staring between his horse's ears, realizing that the prowling cat-men would, doubtless, follow after them; and if another ambush lay ahead, they would be trapped between the two parties. He contented himself with turning his head to Eduin and warning, tersely, "Cat-men ahead. Better be ready."

Then he willed out of his body once more, focused deep on the starstone, and was again floating above the cat-men, studying the tenuous nets of force that hid their bodies from his physical eyes, noting the way those strands fanned out from the shadow. Just where and when could those webs be broken?

He saw it, reflected in the tension of the cat-bodies which he could see clearly in the over-world, when he and his men came into view. He saw them drawing short, curved swords — like claws. And still he waited, till the crouching cat-men came up to their feet and began to run quietly and swiftly over the snow, noiseless on their soft pads. Then he drew deep into the starstone and hurled a sudden blast of energy like a lightning bolt, focused on the carefully spun net of energies, ripping it apart.

Then he was back in his body as the cat-men, not yet realizing that their magical invisibility was gone, came running toward them over the snow. But before he regained full control of his body, his horse reared and screamed in terror, and Damon, reacting a split second too late to the horse's movement, slid off into the snow. He saw one of the cat-men bounding toward him, and felt a tightening surge of something — not quite fear — as he fumbled his hand into the basket-hilt of Dom Esteban's sword.

. . . Miles away, in the Great Hall at Armida, Dom Esteban Lanart stirred in his sleep. His shoulders twitched, and his thin lips curled back in a smile — or a snarl — that had been seen on countless battlefields. . . .

Damon found himself rolling to his feet, his hand whipping the sword from its sheath in a long slash. His point ripped through the white-furred belly and there was blood on the blade outstretched beyond, the blade that was already pointed at a second cat-man.

As that one slashed at his middle, he saw and felt his wrist turn slightly to move his point down, into the path of the cut; as steel rang, he felt his leg jerk in a little kick step, and suddenly his point was buried in the furred throat.

He caught a brief glimpse of Eduin and Rannan, superb horsemen like all the men of the Alton Domain, whirling their frightened horses, slashing down at the gray-furred bodies surrounding them. One went down under a kick from Rannan's horse, but he had no more time to spare for them; wide green eyes glared at him, and a mouth of needlelike fangs opened in a menacing hiss. Tufts of black fur twitched atop the wide ears as the creature whipped its blade around to knock his point aside, and spun on, the scythe-blade flashing toward his eyes. Damon felt a spasm of terror, but his own blade had already whirled at the head; the two swords clashed and he saw a spark leap in the cold. The snarling cat-face lurched forward at him, and for a second he was fighting empty air.

It flickered in and out of visibility; whatever power lurked behind the dark edge of shadow was trying to hide its minions again. Stark terror and despair clawed at him for a moment, so painfully that he half wondered if he had been wounded. Then, with a deep breath, he realized what he had to do, and focused on the starstone. As he abandoned his body wholly to Esteban's skill, he prayed momentarily that the link would hold. Then he forgot his body (either it was safe with Esteban or it wasn't, either way he couldn't help much) and hurled himself upward into the overworld.

The shadow lay blank and terrible before him, and from it questing tendrils were weaving, seeking, to cloak the angry red shadows of the cat-things that fought there.

He reached blindly into the energy-nets and found that without conscious thought he had brought a blade of pure force into his hand. He brought it down on the fine shadow-stuff and the half-woven net of darkness shriveled and burned away. Severed tendrils, quivering, recoiled into the shadow, and their ends faded and vanished. The shadow swirled and eddied, drew back, and out of the midst of the darkness a great cat-face glared at him.

He raised his glowing blade and stood fronting that great menace. Somewhere near his feet he was dimly aware of tiny forms fighting below him, four cats tinier than kittens, three little men, and one of those men . . . surely it was Dom Esteban, surely that was his sidestep, his twirling disengage . . . ?

The dark mist swirled again, veiling the great cat, and now only the glowing eyes and the fierce evil grin stared at him, and somewhere in the back of his mind, a lunatic whisper in Damon's voice muttered half aloud, "I've often seen a cat without a grin, but a grin without a cat . . . ?" and Damon in a split second wondered if he were going mad.

Only two of the little solid cat-things were still on their feet and fighting below him. Unconcerned, he saw one of them go down, spitted on the sword of the man who fought afoot. One of the horsemen struck down the second. The swirling shadow covered the great glaring eyes, their green glow changing, behind the gray wall of mist, to a red glow, like distant, burning coals; then the gray wall blotted them out. A black arrow of force hurled at him and he caught it on his flaming blade. He waited, but the grayness remained, unrippled, even the last glimpse of the glowing cat-eyes gone, and finally he permitted himself to sink earthward, into his body. . . .

There was blood on his sword, and blood on the pale grayish fur of the twisted dead things in the snow. He rested the point of his sword on the ground, and suddenly became aware that he was shaking all over.

Eduin wheeled his horse and rode toward him. He had broken open his face-wound and, from the blue unguent smeared over it to keep out the cold, drops of blood were trickling; otherwise he seemed unhurt. "They're gone," he said, and his voice sounded oddly faraway and weary. "I got the last of them. Will I catch your horse, Lord Damon?"

The sound of his name recalled Damon from a

blind, baseless anger, directed at Eduin, an anger he could not understand. Shaking, he realized he had been about to curse the man, to scream at him with rage for riding down *his* prey, an anger so great that he was shaking from head to foot, with a strange half-memory of charging the last of the cat-men, and the other had thundered past him and stolen the last of the quarry from him.

"Lord Damon!" Eduin's voice was stronger now, and alive with concern. "Are you wounded? What ails you, *vai dom?*"

Damon passed his sweating palm over his forehead. He realized for the first time that there was a scratch, hardly more than a razor-cut, on the back of his left hand. He said, "I've cut myself worse at shaving," and in that instant . . .

In that instant Andrew Carr sat up, shaking his head, sweating and trembling with the memory of what he — *he?* — had done and seen. He had lived through the entire battle in Damon's mind and body.

Damon was safe. And Andrew could keep contact with him — *and* with Callista.

Chapter
TEN

The afternoon clouds were gathering when Damon and his party rode down a narrow and grass-grown roadway toward a little cluster of cottages lying in a valley at the foot of a cliffside.

"Is this the village of Corresanti?" Eduin asked. "I am not overfamiliar with this country-side. And besides" — he scowled — "everything looks strange in this damnable mist. Is it really there — the shadow and darkness — or have they done something to our minds to make us *think* it's darker?"

"I think it's really there," Damon said slowly. "Cats are not sunlight animals but nocturnal ones. It may be that whoever is doing this to these lands feels discomforted by the light of the sun, and has spread a mist over it, to ease the eyes of his people. It's not a complicated piece of work with a starstone, but of course none of our people would want to do it: we have little enough sunlight even in summer."

Not a complicated bit of work. But it takes power. Whoever their cat-adept may be, he has power, and is growing rapidly. If we cannot disarm him swiftly, he may become too powerful for anyone to do so. Our task is to rescue Callista. But if we rescue her and leave these lands lying beneath the shadow, others will suffer. Yet we cannot move against him until Callista is free, or his first act will be to kill her.

He had been half prepared for what he was to see by the memory of Reidel's words — "withered gardens" — but not for any such scene of blight and disaster as met his eyes as he rode past the little houses and farms. The fields lay shadowed beneath the dimmed sun, straggling plants withering in the ground, the drainage ditches fouled and filled with rotting fungus, the great sails of the windmills broken and torn, gaping useless. Here and there, from one of the barns, came the doleful sound of untended and starving beasts. In the middle of the road, almost beneath Eduin's hooves, a ragged child sat listlessly gnawing on a filthy root. As the horsemen passed, he raised his eyes, and Damon thought he had never seen such terror and hopelessness in any face that could vaguely be called human. But the child did not cry. Either he was long past tears or, as Damon suspected, he was simply too weak. The houses seemed deserted, except for blank, listless faces now and again at a window, turned incuriously to the sound of their hooves.

Eduin raised his hands to his face, whispering, "Blessed Cassilda, guard us! I have seen nothing like this since last the trailmen's fever raged in the lowlands! What has come to them?"

"Hunger and terror," Damon said briefly.

"Terror so great that even hunger cannot drive them into the darkened fields." He felt a fury and rage which threatened to spill out into furious cursing, but he clutched at his starstone and deliberately stilled his breathing. Another score against the Great Cat and his minions, the cat-folk he had let loose to amuse themselves in this innocent village.

The other Guardsman, Rannan, had no such aid to calm. He said, and his face looked green with sickness, "Lord Damon, can't we do something for these people — anything?"

Damon said, torn with pity, "Whatever we could do would be a small bandage on a death-wound, Rannan, and we could help them but little before whatever had overcome them turned its strength on us and we joined them, creeping into a doorway to lie down and die in despair. We can only strike at the heart of the cancer, perhaps; and we dare not do that until my kins-woman is safe."

"How do we know she is not dead already, Lord?"

"I will know through the stone," Damon said. It was easier than explaining that Andrew would somehow manage to communicate it. "And I swear to you, if once we hear she is dead, we will turn all our forces to attack and exterminate this whole nest of evil — to the last claw and whisker!" Resolutely he turned his eyes away from the horror of blight and ruin. "Come. First we must reach the caves."

And once there, he thought grimly, *we're likely to have our troubles getting inside, or finding out where belowground they keep Callista hidden.*

He focused his mind on the stone, looking across at the base of the hillside where, he remembered from a boyhood excursion years ago, a great doorway led into the caves of Corresanti. Years ago they had been used for shelter against the severest winters, when snow lay so deep on the Kilghard Hills that neither man nor animal could survive; now they were used for storage of food, for cultivation of edible mushrooms, for the aging of wines and cheeses, and similar uses. Or they had been used for these things until the cat-people came into this part of the world. There should be food stored there, Damon thought, to tide these starving folk over until their next harvest. Unless the cat-folk had destroyed their hoards of food out of sheer wantonness. They could bring the villagers through. Assuming, that was, that they came through themselves.

It seemed to him now that a great and palpable darkness beat outward from the dark edge of the cliff, some miles from them, where the doorway of the caves of Corresanti was hidden. He had been right in his conjecture, then. The caves of Corresanti were the very heart of the shadow, the focus at the heart of the darkening lands. Somewhere in there some monstrous intelligence, not human, experimented blindly with monstrous, unknown power. Damon was a Ridenow, and the

Ridenows had been bred to scent and deal with alien intelligences, and that ancient Gift in his very blood and cells tingled with awareness and terror. But he mastered it, and rode steadily on through the deserted streets of the village.

He looked around, searching for any human face, any sign of life. Was everyone here terrified into insensibility? His eyes fell on a house he knew; he had stayed here one summer, as a boy, so long, so very long ago. He pulled up his horse, a sudden ache clutching his heart.

I haven't seen any of them for years. My foster mother married one of the MacArans, a paxman to Dom Esteban, and I used to come here in the summer. Her sons were my first playmates. Suddenly Damon could stand it no longer. He had to know what fared in that house!

He pulled the horse to a stop and dismounted, tying the horse to the post. Eduin and Rannan called questioningly, but he did not answer; slowly, they dismounted, but did not follow him toward the steps of the cottage. He knocked; only silence followed the knocking, and he pulled the door open. After a moment a man slouched toward the door, his eyes vacant; he cringed away as if by habit. Damon thought, confused, *This is surely one of Alanna's sons. I played with him as a boy, but how changed!* He fumbled for the name. Hjalmar? Estill?

"Cormac," he said at last, and the blank eyes looked up at him, an idiotic smile touching the features briefly.

"*Serva, dom,*" he muttered.

"What has come to you? What — what do they want of you, what is happening here?" Words came tumbling out by themselves. "Do you see the cat-men often? What do they —"

"Cat-men?" the man mumbled, a hint of question in his dull voice. "Not men — women! Cathags . . . they come in the night and tear your soul to ribbons. . . ."

Damon shut his eyes, sickened. Blank-faced, Cormac turned back into the house; the visitors had ceased, for him, to exist. Damon stumbled back into the street, cursing.

The sound of hooves caught his ears; turning, he glimpsed the riders, coming swiftly in single file down a road that ran from a hill above the village. Here in the ruined village they had seen no horses, or cattle, nor any domestic beasts of any kind.

They were near enough now to be clearly seen; they wore shirt-cloaks and breeches of a strange cut, and they were all tall, thin men, with thick, rough pale hair, but they were men. Human men, not cat-folk, unless this was another of the illusions cast. . . .

Damon focused through his starstone, through the dimming haze which still seemed to obscure, like murky water, everything that was not close to him. But these were real men, on real horses. No horse ever foaled would stand quiet for a cat-man to mount. Nor were these the mindless faces of the villagers, terrorized into immobility and apathy.

"Dry-Towners," muttered Eduin. "Lord of Light be with us!"

Now Damon knew where he had seen tall, pale, rangy men like that before. The desert folk rarely penetrated to this part of the world, but now and again he had seen a solitary caravan of them, traveling silent and swift toward their own part of the world.

And our horses are already wearied; if the Dry-Town men are hostile . . . ?

He hesitated. Rannan leaned across to grasp his arm. "What are we waiting for? Let's get out of here!"

"They may not be enemies," Damon began. Surely humans would not join the cat-folk in this plunder and terror?

Eduin's mouth was a grim, set line. "There were small bands of them fighting among the cat-folk last year, and I've heard there were cat-men helping the Dry-Towners in that trouble down Carthon way. They trade with the cat-men, I've heard. Zandru knows *what* they trade, or what they get in return, but the trading's a fact."

Damon's heart sank. They should have fled at once. Too late now, so he made the best of it. "These may be traders," he said, "and have nothing to do with us." In any case they were so close now that the leading Dry-Towner was reining in his mount. "We'll just have to bluff it through; stay ready, but don't draw swords unless I give you the signal, or unless they attack us."

The leader of the Dry-Towners looked down at

209

them, lounging in his saddle, the faint trace of a sneer on his face — or was that just the normal cast of his features? "*Hali-imyn,* by Nebran! Who would have thought it?" His gaze swept over the empty streets. "What are you folk still doing here?"

"Corresanti has been a village of the Alton Domain for more years than Shainsa has stood on the plains," said Damon; he was trying to count the horsemen reined in behind the leader. Six, eight — too many! "I might as well ask you if you are astray from your normal trading paths, and demand you show safe-conduct from the Lord Alton."

"The days of safe-conducts are over in the Kilghard Hills," the leader said. "Before long it will be you folk who learn you must ask leave to ride here." His teeth bared in a lazy grin. He slid from his horse, the men behind him following suit. Damon's hand slid into the basket-hilt of his sword, and the small matrix there felt smooth and hot in his palm. . . .

. . . Dom Esteban laid down the meat-roll he had been eating, and leaned back against his pillow, his eyes wide, staring. The servant who had brought him the food spoke to him, but he did not reply. . . .

"It will be long before I ask leave to ride in my kinsmen's lands," Damon said. "But what are *you* doing here?" His voice sounded oddly shrill and weak in his own ears.

"We?" said the Dry-Towner. "Why, we're

peaceful traders, aren't we, comrades?" There was a chorus of assent from the men behind him. They did not look particularly peaceful (*Of course*, Damon thought in a split second, *Dry-Towners never did*), their swords jutting from their hips at an aggressive angle ready to draw, swaggering like tavern brawlers. The horses behind them began to paw the ground nervously, and frightened snorts filled the air.

"Peaceful traders," insisted the leader, fumbling with the clasp of his shirt-cloak, "trading here by permission of the Lord of these lands, who has given us a few small commissions." The hand whipped out of his shirt-cloak, holding a long ugly knife, and then he jerked his long, straight sword free of its sheath. "Throw down your weapons," he grated, "and if you're fool enough to think you can resist, look behind you!"

Eduin's hand caught Damon's arm in an agonizing grip. Out of the corner of his eye, a quick backward-flipped glance over the shoulder, Damon saw why. Out of the thick forest at the edge of the road, spreading out behind the three Guardsmen to cut them off, cat-men were padding quietly on large, soft paws. Too many cat-men. Damon couldn't begin to count them and didn't try. He found that Dom Esteban's sword was in his hand, but despair took him. Even Dom Esteban could never fight his way out of such an ambush!

The Dry-Towners were closing in slowly, knife

and sword in each hand. Damon had forgotten the dagger hanging at his own belt; he was startled as his left hand plucked it out and extended it toward the enemy. He found himself in a stance almost the direct opposite of the one he had been trained to, looking over his left shoulder at his foe past the point of the extended dagger, his sword-hilt cold against his right cheek. *Of course. Esteban had traveled beyond the Dry-Towns, knew how the desert people fought. . . .*

He thought, coldly, that there must have been an ambush back there. If they had mounted and fled, as the Dry-Towners must have expected, they would have ridden straight into the cat-men.

"Take them!" the Dry-Town leader snarled.

There was no escape; the alternatives were death or surrender. Damon's mind hung undecided, not knowing what to do, but his body knew. As the two blades of the Dry-Towner came at him Damon saw the tip of his own sword dip suddenly, sweeping sharply across the sword and dagger, driving them aside; felt his feet shift and his body dip.

So Dom Esteban thinks we can cut down ten men and get away, he thought, ironic and detached, watching somehow without involvement as his sword and dagger drove both points at the same time into the Dry-Town leader's side. He heard the clatter of steel on both sides of him, and saw another one circling toward his back.

His head turned and as his sword jerked free a

simple motion of his forearm brought it around. The other man, running, had let his guard slip. Damon felt his own weight shift suddenly, and then his sword went between the man's ribs. He caught a glimpse of Eduin, his sword red in the last glare of sunlight, running to meet another man who was falling back, fear on his face . . . and then he was spinning away, dagger lifting to fend off a thrust that had been coming straight at his throat. His sword flashed at an elbow and the Dry-Towner was screaming at his feet and Damon's stomach turned at the sight of the raw horror where the man's arm had been torn half through. . . .

"They're demons," one of the Dry-Towners shouted. "They're not men at all. . . ." Damon saw that the Dry-Towners still alive were falling back, jostling up against the restive horses which made a wall behind them. They had never seen five men die that fast before. . . .

Demons . . . the Dry-Towners were known to be a superstitious lot. . . .

One of the remaining Dry-Towners shouted something in his own language, trying to rally his remaining comrades, and ran toward Eduin. Damon ignored him, diving deep into the focus of the starstone, even noticing the man's hand was too high. . . . Damon's body whirled and stepped, and his sword went between the man's elbows, slicing so expertly that it touched no bone, and the man fell. Damon himself did not notice. He reached deep into his subconscious, into the dark closet where he had locked away the nightmares of his childhood, and brought forth a demon. It was gray and scaly, horned and taloned, smoke and flame gushing from its nostrils; he hurled the picture into the lens of the starstone, focusing it between him and the Dry-Towners. . . .

The Dry-Towners screamed and ran, trying to catch their wildly plunging horses, which were now running wild, maddened by the smell of blood and the musk of cat. Wild screeching rose from the cat-men behind them. Damon pictured — knowing they all saw — the demon turning, charging down the village street toward the cat-people, roaring, fire shooting from its mouth and nostrils. Some of the cat-men broke and ran. Others, perhaps sensing it was not quite what it seemed, tried to dodge around it.

Damon reached blindly for the bridle of his horse; the rearing, fear-maddened beast kicked and plunged, but Damon, his mind still on the demon he had set off ravening among the cat-men (it was stalking them now, reaching out right and left with a great stench of burning cat-fur), found himself tearing the reins loose and vaulting to the saddle with a command of horsemanship as much beyond his own as — *as Dom Esteban's, of course.*

One of the cat-men was too close, and he had to guard against a slash from the deadly claw-curved sword. He lopped at it; saw sword and paw fall together, twitching convulsively, and lie still. He never saw what happened to the cat-man's body; he was already pulling his horse around.

Something like a lightning bolt struck the gray-scaled monster Damon had created, and it flared up in a column of gray dust and smoke and vanished. Damon's mind reeled with horrid shock.

It was Esteban who guided the terrified horse, who cut down the few cat-men who ran at the beast's heels and tried to hamstring him, who guided the horse along the road upward to the caves. Dimly, distantly, Damon knew what Esteban was doing with his body and his horse, but he himself was flying above the overworld, borne swiftly and unwillingly through ever-thickening, boiling mist toward the black heart of the shadow, from which glared, unveiled, and blazing out like the fires at the heart of a volcano, the terrible eyes of the Great Cat.

With the eyes, blazing and scorching, were claws, claws that reached, snatched at Damon where he wheeled and turned, dodging, evading them. Damon knew that if even the tip of one of those deadly claws touched him, raked into his heart, he would be forced back into his body and the Great Cat could do with that as he would, blast him lifeless with a single scorching breath.

Damon thought, *What are cats afraid of?* His body, in the overworld, shot up; he dropped on all fours, and knew that where he had flown and dodged from the claws of the cat, now a great, wavering dark wolf-shape grew and solidified before the cat. He plunged at the cat, hearing the terrifying werewolf-howl reverberating through the overworld, a paralyzing cry before which the cat-thing dimmed and wavered for a moment. A scorching breath seared the wolf's eyes, and he howled with rage as Damon felt himself tremble with the blood-lust. He flung himself at the throat of the cat-thing, great dripping jaws closing, the teeth of the werewolf-thing fastening over the cat's throat, the stink of cat-musk —

The great furred threat thinned and vanished from between the teeth; Damon heard himself howl again and tried to spring at the darkness, maddened with the insane hunger to tear, to bite, to feel the blood burst out under his fangs. . . .

But the cat was gone, melted away, and Damon, shaking and drained, sick to his very toenails, and retching with the taste of blood in his throat, sat swaying in his saddle. The cat-adept had been forced off the astral plane by Damon's werewolf-form. For the first time, it looked as if the Great Cat might not be invulnerable, after all. For the road lay bare ahead to the caves, with nothing before them except bodies of the dead.

Chapter
ELEVEN

A brief sharp shock, like the shock of falling, brought Andrew Carr awake. The brief winter day was waning, the room was dim, and by the fading light of the window he saw Callista at the foot of his bed. He saw for a moment, with relief, that she was dressed in a skirt and loose tunic, and her hair braided. No, it was Ellemir, and she had a tray of food in her hands. She said, "Andrew, you must eat something."

"I'm not hungry," Andrew muttered, still disoriented with sleep and confused dreams — giant cats? Werewolves? How did it fare with Damon? Was Callista still safe? How could he have slept? How could Ellemir speak of food at a time like this?

"No, you must," Ellemir said, accurately following his thoughts. That would take some getting used to. Well, he'd better get used to it, he told himself.

She sat down on the edge of the bed and said, "Matrix work is terribly draining; you must keep up your strength or you'll overload. I knew you wouldn't feel like it, so I brought you some soup, and things like that which are easy to swallow. I know how you feel, but *try*, Andrew." She said, shrewdly, the one thing which would have persuaded him.

"Damon cannot reach Callista. Once inside the caves of Corresanti, he may not be able to find her in the darkness; it's a dreadful labyrinth of dark passages. I was there once, and I heard of a man who wandered there until he came out months later, blinded and with his hair turned white with fear. So you must be ready when he needs you, to guide him toward Callista. And for that you must be strong."

Reluctantly, but convinced by her argument, Andrew picked up the spoon. It was a meat soup with long noodles in it, very strong and good. With it was a nut bread and sharp jelly. Once he tasted it, he realized that he was half starved and he ate up everything on the tray.

"How is your father?" he asked for courtesy's sake.

She giggled faintly. "You should have seen the meal *he* put away an hour or so ago, telling me between bites how many cat-men he had killed —"

Andrew said soberly, "I saw it. I was *there*. They are terrible!" He shuddered, knowing that part of what he thought a dream had been his mind wandering among the villages blighted by the shadow of the Great Cat. He put down the last bread crust. Briefly, turning his mind inward to the starstone and the contact with Damon, he saw them . . . nearing the caves, the slope clear before them. . . .

This time it was easier to step into the over-world, and because the dim light of the winter day was fading, he discovered that he could see better in the dim blue glimmer of what Callista had called the "overlight." Blue? he thought. Was that because the stones were blue and somehow cast the light through his mind? He looked down at himself and saw his body slumped back on the bed, and Ellemir, setting the tray on the floor, knelt beside him and laid her hand on his body's pulse as she had done with Damon.

He realized briefly that in the overworld he had left behind the heavy fur-and-leather garments he had borrowed from Ellemir's servant, and was wearing the thin gray nylon tunic and trousers he wore around the office at Terran HQ, with the narrow band of jewels on his collar, eight of them, one for each planet where he had seen service.

Damn cold for this planet. Oh, hell, this is the overworld. If Callista can go around in her torn nightie without freezing to death, what difference does it make? He realized that he had moved an immense distance from Ellemir and he was outside Armida, on a gray and featureless plain with distant, shimmery, miragelike hills in the distance. *Now, which way to the caves of Corresanti?* he asked himself, trying to orient himself in the gray distances, and as if by the wings of thought he found himself borne swiftly over the spaces between.

He found that between his fingers he still held the starstone, or rather whatever referent to it existed in the overworld, and that here it gleamed like a firework, sending off brilliant sparkles of fire. He wondered if it would take him directly toward Callista. Yes, he was moving, and now he could see the hills clearly, a great darkness seeming to emanate from their very center. Was it behind that darkness that Damon had seen the Great Cat? Was it he who held Callista captive beneath the great illegal matrix jewel?

Andrew shuddered, trying not to think of the Great Cat. Or rather, to transform him, in his thoughts, to the Cheshire cat of Terran children's tales, the great harmless cat which grinned enormously and made amusing conversation. Or Puss-in-Boots. *He's just a character out of a fairy tale,* Andrew told himself, *and I'm damned if I'll let him get on my nerves.* Instinctively he knew that was the safest way to protect himself from the power of the Great Cat. *Puss in Boots,* he reminded himself. *I hope Damon doesn't meet him again. . . .*

As if the thought of Damon had given him a definite direction, he discovered that he was standing (though his feet were not quite touching the ground) on a slope just outside a great dark cave-mouth, and a little below him, Damon and his two men, swords drawn and ready, were slowly working their way toward the cave-mouth. He tried to wave to him, to make Damon see him, and then that curious *merging* happened again; and again he was seeing out from behind Damon's eyes. . . .

. . . Scarcely breathing, placing his feet as silently as possible. *As we had to do, scouting, in the campaigns last year. . . .*

He could see the great indolent cats sprawled before the entrance of the cave, drowsing at their post; secure in their faith that the Power they served would guard them in return.

But they were still cats, and their great tufted ears lifted suddenly at the soft brushing of boots through grass, and instantly they were on their feet, the claw-swords ready. Damon found himself leaping forward, sword already alive in his hand, driving toward the nearest in a long lunge. The cat's curved blade whipped down in that curious, circling guard they used, blurring to a half-moon before its body, driving his point down and away, and Damon saw bright steel flash toward his side.

Then he was looking at the back of his wrist as his arm jerked up, and felt the blade trembling in his hand as the other struck its earth-aimed point; he heard its edge hissing past his ear as it whirled around his body, slashing at the furred shoulder. The cat-man's sword lifted to meet it; he leaped back, and saw the blurred point of the scythe-sword slice the air an inch in front of his eyes. The great circling blows of the curved blade looked clumsy, and yet it seemed to take all Esteban's skill to find a weakness in that whirling defense. Eduin and Rannan were engaged nearby — he heard their swords clashing and battering behind him. He felt his arm snap forward in a feint — he knew it was a feint because his feet did not move. The curved claw-sword whistled down; Dom Esteban's sword dropped out of its path, whirling back and up, and came down between the tufted ears.

He jerked his sword from the bloody skull with an expert tug and ran to where Rannan, his shirt ripped and wet with blood, was falling back before one of the whirling blades. His own blade whirled and danced, raining cut after cut at the creature's head. He jumped back from a great whistling stroke that could have sliced him in half at the waist, felt the blade coming around in an enormous circling cut that he thought was another head cut, until he felt his wrist drop and the long, thin blade sliced through the cat-creature's knee. His arm jerked again and as the squalling creature fell forward the point jabbed into its throat. Eduin and Rannan were standing over the lifeless body of the last of the guards and again, for an instant, Damon felt that same strange baseless surge of Dom Esteban's anger. . . .

Damon shook his head. He felt oddly dizzy, as if he were drunk. What was he doing? He opened his eyes and sheathed his sword, aware as he did so of aching muscles at the base of his thumb and in his wrist: muscles he'd never known he had. Swaying a little, he turned his back on the grisly heaps of bloody fur lying on the ground, and tottered toward the cave-mouth, motioning to Eduin and Rannan to follow. As he ran, he saw a strange man's form before him, clad in thin, gray unfamiliar clothing. It was a moment before he recognized Andrew Carr . . . and as the realization of who it was came into Damon's mind, Andrew was back in his own mind again, standing a few feet away from Damon and motioning him forward.

It seemed a little strange to Andrew to be able to see Damon when Damon was not in the overworld, but after all, he, "down there," had seen Callista. He stepped ahead of him into the entrance of the cave. It was a great dark chamber, and for a moment, even in the overlight, it was hard to see. Damon was through the doorway now and was motioning, impatiently, for his swordsmen to follow; they seemed to be pressing against some barrier invisible to Andrew — and evidently invisible to Damon, too.

For a moment the Darkovan looked puzzled, then — and neither then nor later did Andrew know whether Damon spoke aloud or whether he heard him *thinking* — Damon said, "Oh, of course. There's a first-level barrier across the entrance, which means no one can get in and out unless either he's carrying a matrix, or the operator *lets* him in or out." Of course. It was just what the Great Cat would do. But it might mean an extra vulnerability. He couldn't be everywhere at once, even with a matrix. But if they were lucky, he might not know that yet.

Slowly, Damon moved through the huge vaulted chamber which was the entrance to the caves. Somewhere at the back he heard water dripping, and his eyes saw only the little bit of daylight admitted from the cave-mouth, which faded as he went farther. The cold terror of the dark was on him, and he hesitated, remembering, *When I came here as a boy, there were torches, there were lights mounted by which we could see the walls and the pathways.* Then he saw, seemingly emerging from the very wall itself, the spectral figure of Andrew. The Earthman's figure seemed to glow with faint blue light, and between his hands he bore what looked like a great sparkling blue torch. *The matrix, of course. Will it alert that cat-thing? If I must go into the overworld, to find my way, will he see my starstone?*

Now he seemed to hear a droning, humming sound, like some gigantic hive of bees. Out of the dim chambers of memory, he recognized it now: a powerful, unshielded matrix. A cold spasm of fear squeezed his heart in an iron band that was almost physical pain. *That cat-thing must be mad! Mad or more powerful than any man or any Keeper! It would take a Circle of at least four minds to handle a matrix-screen that size!*

They never came that way in nature. They had made them artificially, in the heyday of starstone technology. Had he found this one, a freak, or could he have *made* it? *How in Zandru's nine hells does he handle the thing? I wouldn't touch it for my life!* Damon thought.

Again he saw Andrew's figure, beckoning dimly in the bluish glow. By the light of his starstone, he saw massive crystalline pillars, great stony spikes that jutted from floor to ceiling or down from ceiling to floor. Everywhere was the dark dampness and the sound of falling water, and the terrifying drone of the matrix. Damon thought he could find his way down to it by sound alone. But that would come later. Right now he had to find Callista and get her out of here before the cat-thing knew he was here and sent one of his henchmen to cut her throat.

At the back of the chamber two passages ran back into darkness and dim far-off glimmers. He paused a moment, irresolute, before seeing, far down the left hand passage, the form of Andrew Carr. He followed the dim spectral figure, and after stumbling twice on the rocky floor — of course, Andrew in the overworld couldn't stub his toes — he focused on his own starstone, warm and heavy and naked against his throat, to focus a ball of witchlight in front of him. It was hard and sluggish and Damon suspected that its power was being damped by proximity to the enormous one nearby, but he did manage to focus enough power to make a little light. *Damn good thing too. How could I fight my way through, in case I have to, and hold a torch in my other hand?*

Andrew's figure had vanished again, going far ahead. *Yes, that was right. He should find Callista. Tell her help's on the way,* Damon reasoned.

In the shadow beyond the faint witchlight something moved, and a voice spoke in the mewing speech of the cat-men. The voice changed to a sudden snarl. Damon saw one of the curved blades flash outside the circle of light. The droning in his head was maddening, painful. He drew out his sword, raised it, but it seemed a dead, awkward weight in his hand. *Dom Esteban* . . . he reached frantically for that contact, but there was nothing, only that droning, blurring sound, that *pain.*

The curved blade came whistling down. Somehow he got the inert metal thing in his hand aloft, into the path of the cut, a barrier of steel. Fear choked him as he forced his weary body into stance, parrying automatically, not daring to expose himself to attack. He was alone, fighting with only his own meager skill!

The barrier at the cave-mouth! Dom Esteban couldn't reach him through it! And he thought, *I'm dead!*

In a split second he remembered years of tedious lessons — always the worst swordsman in his age-group, the clumsy boy, the one never meant for the arts of war. The coward. Feeling sluggish with terror, feeling as if his sword dragged through thick syrup, he parried the skilled, circling strokes. He was doomed. He could not defend himself adequately against men fighting in the style to which he was trained. How then could he stand against these masters of a wholly alien technique? He backed away frantically, seeing out of the corner of his eye that a second guard was running to join the first, and in a moment he would face two of them — if he lived that long. He saw the terrible scythe-blade spinning in a blow he could never have caught, even though he knew how Esteban would have blocked it.

The blade came up in the deft block he had pictured, and, with a wild thrill of relief he saw the weakness in the cat-man's position, and at the same instant drove his sword into it. The second guard ran up just as Damon, gasping, pulled his sword free. He turned to face it, knowing perfectly well how Esteban would attack this one, and as the thought formed in his mind his arm jabbed out, back; the claw-sword whirred down in that circling guard they all seemed to use; Damon launched himself in a long lunge, piercing the furred throat even as the sickle-sword reversed, striking his blade weakly in a feeble attempt to guard.

He whipped the sword free, and the third cat-guard stopped crouching warily, and began to back away across the cave floor, its down-curved blade poised beside its head, ready to sweep down in that strange, spinning defense. Damon stepped toward it, warily, and waited. . . .

Seconds crawled by, and his body did nothing he didn't tell it to. He focused on the link . . . nothing. Only the pulsing, throbbing overload from the giant matrix, somewhere down deep in the cave, out of sight, almost out of knowledge, but there, present, dreadful. Dom Esteban could not reach him here. *Had not* reached him here. Damon nearly dropped his sword as realization shocked him. He had not been in touch with Esteban at all, yet he had killed two of the cat-men.

And he would kill a third. Now.

Why not? He had always understood all the tricks, he had been taught by master swordsmen, even though the practice eluded him . . . perhaps that was the problem. He had thought about life more than he had lived it, always his body and his mind had been separated; perhaps the contact with Esteban had taught his nerves and muscles directly how to react. . . .

The cat-man snarled and launched itself at him, and he hurled himself down, sword extended before him, catching himself with his other hand on the floor. The claw-sword hissed above his head, a clean miss, and something wet and sticky gushed over his arm. He pulled his own sword free with a sharp tug and raised himself. Now which way to Callista? Quickly, before the Great Cat finds . . .

He looked around for Andrew, and saw him, a split second flash at the far end of the passage, and then Andrew was gone. . . .

Andrew, wrapped up, sharing the battle with Damon, suddenly heard something like a cry, and in a flash he saw Callista. It seemed that she was lying on the floor at his feet — and he realized abruptly that he had moved far down, into a deeper level of the caves, where the walls glowed faintly with pale greenish phosphorescence. Callista was lying in the darkness, but as she opened terrified eyes, Andrew saw, sneaking toward her and only a dim shadowy form in the darkness, the form of one of the cat-creatures. Callista scrambled to her feet and backed away, helplessly defending herself with her outthrust arms. The cat-thing had a curved dagger in its paws, and Andrew ran toward it helplessly, struggling.

I need my body, I cannot defend her from the overworld. . . . For an instant he wavered between the cave where Callista blindly fled from the cat-man's knife, between the upper room at Armida where his body lay guarded by Ellemir, back and forth, struggling, torn. *I cannot go back, I must stay with Callista. . . .* Then there was a blue flash and a painful, dazzling electrical shock, and Andrew felt himself drop hard on his feet in the cave, in pitch-dark except for the glow of fungus, his ankle twisting as he came down.

He yelled a warning, ran blindly toward the cat-thing. (*How did I get here? How? Am I really here at all?*) He stumbled, his toes agonizingly banged on loose rock. He scooped up the rock; the cat-man whirled, snarling, but Andrew raised the rock and brought it down hard against the thing's temple. It fell heavily, with an ear-splitting yowl, twitched feebly, and lay still. The force of the blow had spilled its brains all over the floor; Andrew found himself slipping in

229

them and almost falling.

He said, idiotically, "I guess that settles that, I really *am* here." Then he ran toward Callista, who was crouched against the wall, staring up at him in wonder and terror.

"Darling," he cried out. "Callista — darling — are you all right? Have they hurt you?" He caught her in his arms, and she fell heavily against him. She was solid and real and warm in his arms, and he held her hard, feeling her whole body shake with deep, terrifying sobs.

"Andrew — Andrew — it's really you," she repeated.

He pressed his mouth to her wet cheek and repeated again, "It's me, and you're safe now, beloved. We'll have you out of here in a few minutes — can you walk?"

"I can walk," she said, recovering a little of her composure. "I don't know my way out, but I have heard there are ropes along the walls; we can feel our way along and come at last to the entrance. If you will give me the starstone, I can make a light," she said, remembering it at last, and Andrew gently took it out and handed it to her. She cupped it almost tenderly between her palms. In the pale blue light of the stone, paler than the overworld light but still enough to show him quite clearly in its radiance, her lovely delicate features were contorted with fear.

"Damon," she whispered. "Oh, no — Andrew! Andrew, help me —" and in a single moment her fingers reached out for his hand and her thoughts were linked with his as they had been before.

Then, with another of those harsh, painful electric shocks, he was standing on the floor of a great, partially lighted cave chamber, at the far end of which glowed, with a painful radiance, a jewel like the starstone — but a huge one, glowing and sparkling like an arclight, hurting his eyes. Damon, looking very small, was striding toward it, and then Andrew's mind flowed into Damon's again, and he saw, through Damon's eyes, the crouching figure kneeling behind the great stone. Its paws were blackened, and its whiskers scorched away, and huge patches of fur had been singed from its hide. Damon raised his blade —

And found himself in the overworld, while before him, towering in majesty and menace, the Great Cat, taller than a tree, glared down at him, with great red eyes like giant coals, and snarled, a great space-filling roar. It raised one paw and Damon flinched, feeling how the stroke of that paw would fling him aside like a feeble mouse. . . .

At that moment Callista cried out, and two giant dogs — one huge and bull-throated, the other slender and whippet-quick — with great gleaming fangs, leaped at the cat-thing's throat and began worrying it, snarling. *Andrew and Callista!* Without stopping to think, Damon dropped back into his body and ran forward, whipping up his sword. He lunged down on the prone, crouching cat-creature, feeling the droning rise to a scream, to wild snarling howls, to confused yelps and spitting hisses that filled all space. The sword wobbled as Damon, holding it steady with all his might, his hands scorching and seared, ran Dom Esteban's sword through the body of the cat-thing.

It screeched and writhed, screaming, on the sword. The great matrix flared and spat sparks and great sheets of flame. Then abruptly the lights died and the cavern was dull and silent, except for the pale glimmer of Callista's starstone. The three of them were standing close together on the stone floor, Callista sobbing shakily and clinging to them. On the floor at their feet a burned and blackened thing lay, scorched and stinking of burning fur, which bore only the faintest resemblance to a cat-man, or to anything else which had ever been alive.

The great matrix stood before them in its frame, with a burned, dead, glassy glimmer. It rolled free, fell with a tinkle to the floor of the cave, and shattered into nothingness.

Chapter
TWELVE

"So what will happen to the darkening lands now?" Andrew asked, as they rode slowly back through the dusk toward Armida.

"I'm not sure," Damon said slowly. He was very weary, and drooped in his saddle, but he felt at peace.

They had found food and wine in the caves — evidently the cat-men had not bothered to explore the lower levels — and had eaten and drunk well. There had been clothing there, too, of a sort, including great fur blankets, but Callista had shuddered away from the touch, saying that nothing would induce her to wear fur again as long as she lived. In the end Damon had given the fur cloak to Eduin and wrapped Callista in the swordsman's heavy wool cape.

She rode now on the front of Andrew's saddle, clinging to him, her head against his shoulder, and he rode with his head lowered so that his cheek lay against her hair. The sight made Damon lonely for Ellemir, but that could wait. He wasn't sure Andrew even heard the answer to his question, but he answered, anyway.

"Now that the matrix is destroyed, the cat-men have no abnormal weapons of fear or darkness. We can send out soldiers against them and cut them down. The villagers, most of them, will recover when the darkness is gone and there is no more fear."

Below them, in the valley, Damon could see the lights of Armida. He wondered if Ellemir knew he was returning, with Callista safe, and the darkening lands cleansed. Damon smiled faintly. The old man must be fretting himself sick with impatience to know what had happened since he lost contact with Damon at the barrier. Dom Esteban probably believed — he had been contemptuous of Damon for so long as a weakling — that he, Damon, had been cut down seconds after. Well, it would be a pleasant surprise for the old man, and Dom Esteban would need a few pleasant surprises to make up for the inevitable shock he'd get when he found out about Callista and Andrew. That wasn't going to be pleasant, but the old man owed them something, and Damon was going to twist his arm until he gave in. He realized, with a deep and profound pleasure, that he was looking forward to it, that he wasn't afraid of Dom Esteban anymore. He wasn't afraid of *anything* anymore. He smiled, and dropped back to ride by Eduin and Rannan, who shared a horse's broad back, having given up a mount to Andrew and Callista.

Andrew Carr did not even notice Damon go. Callista was warm in his arms, and his heart was so full that he could hardly think clearly. He whispered, "Are you cold, beloved?"

She nestled closely against him. "A little," she said softly. "It's all right."

"It won't be long, and we'll have you where it's warm, and Ellemir will look after you."

"I'd rather be cold in the clean air, than be warm in those foul, stinking caves! Oh, the stars!" she said almost ecstatically.

He tightened his arm around her, aware that she was so weary that she might fall. He could see the lights of Armida, warm and beckoning, below.

She murmured, "It won't be easy. My father will be angry. He thinks of me as a Keeper, not a woman. And he would be angry if I chose to lay down my post and marry anyone, anyone at all, and it will be that much harder, since you are a Terran." But she smiled and curled closer to him. "Well, he'll just have to get used to the idea. Leonie will be on our side."

They were taking it all for granted, Andrew thought. Somehow, he would have to send a message to the Trade City that he was alive — that would be easy enough — and a message that he wouldn't be coming back. That wouldn't be so easy. With this new ability he had discovered — well, somehow or other he'd have to learn how to use it. After that — well, who could tell? There must be something he could do, to hasten the day when Terrans and Darkovans no longer looked on each other as alien species.

They *couldn't* be so alien. The names alone must tell him that. Callista. Damon. Eduin. Caradoc. Esteban. He could buy a lot of coincidence, but that he couldn't believe in. He wasn't a linguist, but he simply refused to accept that these people could independently have evolved names so identical with Terran names. Even *Ellemir* was not outlandish; the first time he heard it, he'd thought it was *Eleanor.* Not only Terran names, but Western European ones, from the days when those distinctions applied on Terra.

Yet this planet had been discovered by the Terran Empire less than a hundred years ago, and the Trade City built less than fifty years ago. The little he knew about this planet showed him that its history was longer than that of the Empire.

So what was the answer? There were stories of "Lost Ships," taking off from Terra itself in the days before the Empire, thousands of years ago, disappearing without trace. Most of them had been believed destroyed — the ships of those days had been ridiculous contraptions, running on primitive atomic or matter-antimatter drives. But one of them *might* somehow have survived. He faced the fact that he'd probably never know, but he had the rest of his life to find out. Anyway, did it matter? He knew all he needed to know.

He clasped Callista closer in his arms; she made a small involuntary movement of protest, then smiled and deliberately moved against him.

He thought, *I really know nothing about her.* Then, remembering that incredible four-way moment of fusion and total acceptance, he realized that he knew all he needed to know about her, too. Already he had noticed that she no longer shrank from a casual touch. He thought, with great tenderness, that if she had been conditioned against desire or sensual response, at least the conditioning was not irrevocable, and they had time enough to wait. Already, he suspected, it had been breached by days of terror alone in the darkness, and by her hunger for any other human presence. But they already belonged to one another in the way that mattered most. The rest would come in time. He was sure of that, and he found himself wondering, whimsically, if precognition was among the new psi talents he'd be exploring.

As they rode through the great looming gates of Armida, a light snow had begun to fall; and Andrew remembered that less than a week ago he had been lying on a ledge in a howling storm, waiting to die.

Callista shivered — did she remember it too? — and he bent down and murmured tenderly, "We're almost home, my beloved." And already it did not seem strange to think of it as home.

He had followed a dream, and it had brought him here.

Author's Note
On Chronology

I am always being asked by those who have read anywhere from three to nine of the Darkover books to tell them exactly when and where any given book fits, chronologically, into the series. While I am always grateful for the interest of my readers, usually the only answer I can give is a shrug. I have always tried to make each of the Darkover books so complete that each one can be read by itself, even if the reader has never seen any of the other books before.

I do not really think of them as a "series" but rather of Darkover as a familiar world about which I like writing novels, and to which the readers seem to like returning. Where absolute consistency might damage the self-sufficiency of any given book, I have quite frankly sacrificed consistency. I make no apologies for this.

Nothing is more frustrating to me than to read the second, or fourth, or sixth book of a series, and to have the author blandly assume that I have read all his other books and know the whole background. When readers start nit-picking, demanding to know (for instance) why two loca-

238

tions are a day's journey apart in one book, and three days' ride in another, I begin to understand why Conan Doyle attempted to throw Sherlock Holmes over the Reichenbach falls, and why Sax Rohmer repeatedly tried to burn, drown, or dismember Fu Manchu so thoroughly that even the publishers could not resurrect him for another book.

But for those who have followed, or tried to follow, the chronology of the Terrans on Darkover, I think of this book as coming perhaps thirty years before STAR OF DANGER while Lorill Hastur still ruled Comyn Council and while Valdir Alton, a younger brother of Ellemir and Callista, was away at Council. Readers of the earlier books will remember that Valdir's adolescent son, Kennard, played an important part in STAR OF DANGER; that Valdir and his Terran foster-son Larry Montray reappeared in WINDS OF DARKOVER, about four years after the previous book. Kennard, grown to manhood, was an important character in THE BLOODY SUN.

Lerrys Ridenow — a grandson, perhaps, of the *Damon* in this book — appeared, with Regis Hastur, in THE PLANET SAVERS. Regis Hastur appeared again, with Lew Alton, son of Kennard, in THE SWORD OF ALDONES; and yet again, as a major character, in WORLD WRECKERS, which was, so far, the last in chronology of the novels. Some general sense of the elapsed time may be gained by the knowledge that Desideria, who appears in WINDS OF DARKOVER as a girl of sixteen, appears (as a minor character) in WORLD WRECKERS as a woman of great age, possibly over a hundred years old.

The books were not written in chronological order. SWORD OF ALDONES, late in the series, was actually written first. DARKOVER LANDFALL, which dealt with how the planet was colonized, long before the coming of the Terran Empire, was actually written *after* WORLD WRECKERS, which otherwise was the last in the series. I prefer to think of it as a loosely interrelated group of novels with a common background — the Terran Empire against the world and culture of Darkover — and a common theme: the clash of two warring cultures, apparently irreconcilable and in spite of all, closely akin. If the books have any message at all, which I personally doubt, it is simply that for a man nothing of mankind is alien.

Marion Zimmer Bradley